SEAL TEAM FOUR

SEAL's Surprise Daughter

Protecting His Brother's Babies

Protecting His New Family

The SEAL's Convenient Marriage

SEAL's Christmas Daughter

SEAL's Justice

RELAY PUBLISHING EDITION, OCTOBER 2020
Copyright © 2020 Relay Publishing Ltd.

Katie Knight is a pen name created by Relay Publishing for co-authored Romance projects. Relay Publishing works with incredible teams of writers and editors to collaboratively create the very best stories for our readers.

Cover design by Mayhem Cover Creations.

www.relaypub.com

PROTECTING

His Brother's Babies

LESLIE NORTH PRESENTS

KATIE KNIGHT

BLURB

My toughest mission may be protecting my own heart…

I'm only in town for one reason: to settle my twin brother's estate.

I didn't come looking to score.

And definitely not with Layla Bailey, my cutthroat brother's ex.

But when she shows up at my door, my gut clenches.

She's just so beautiful. And she needs my help.

She thinks Devon was murdered…and she may be next.

I can't let anything happen to Layla or the baby she's carrying.

My brother's baby.

I promise to keep her safe…which is all I have to offer.

I've got no time for romance. My life is with the SEALs.

Once the danger passes, I'm gone.

Then…Layla kisses me.

Suddenly, I'm thinking crazy thoughts.

Like maybe sticking around wouldn't be so bad after all.

But only if we make it out of this alive…

Great News! *Protecting His Brother's Babies* has been updated on May 7, 2024 and is now part of an exciting new six book series called *SEAL Team Four*. There is an overarching storyline about the SEAL team and is concluded by a sixth brand new novel that will explore their former SEAL leader called *SEAL's Justice*.

ONE

DRAKE

G od. Who the hell needed twenty pairs of the same identical fancy black socks?

I swore under my breath and shook my head, tossing them all in a large box marked "Charity". The excess was par for the course, I supposed, where my twin brother was concerned. Devon had always been far too slick and ostentatious for his own good.

In the end, it was probably what had gotten him killed, wrapping his expensive car around a tree because he'd believed that speed limits were meant for other people. Devon was reckless and rarely thought of the consequences of his actions—he always assumed that someone else would come along to handle the fallout from any of his stunts.

It had only been a week since the car accident that had taken my brother's life, but already my neat, orderly life had been upended more than I could have imagined. And from the call I'd gotten earlier from the attorney for my family's company, things would only get worse before they got better.

No. "Company" didn't begin to cover what had become the Shepperton, Inc. manufacturing empire over the years. It was a behemoth, a massive industrial player with thousands of employees. And that meant that no matter how badly I wanted to walk away from the whole thing, I had to step up, take charge, and make sure the business was properly transitioned to new leadership now that my brother was no longer at the helm.

That much was my duty as a Shepperton—even if it was a duty that I'd dodged for the past several years. I'd inherited the business along with Devon five years ago after our parents died, but I'd had exactly zero interest in leaving behind my hard-won career as a SEAL to share management of a business I hated. Devon had been more than happy to have the top seat at the company to himself, and I had been happy to leave him to it. Dividends from my shares were automatically deposited into an account that I never even looked at. An account that would grow even larger once Devon's assets were added to it.

I didn't care about the money. I would give it all up if it meant getting back the people that I'd lost in the last year. There never would have been a good time to lose Devon, but timing made it sting even more. I was coming up on the one-year anniversary of losing one of my teammates in action. Kyle Cuddy, all of twenty-two, just a kid who should have had so much life ahead of him. And Devon, the last tie I had to my family and my home. We weren't close—but now we'd never get the chance to be. And that hurt like hell.

I continued going through my brother's clothes and other personal effects, separating out what I could send to charity and disposing of the rest in preparation for putting Devon's million-dollar mini-palace of a condo on the market.

I could have kept it all, according to my brother's will. Hell, I probably *should* keep at least some of the clothes—they'd fit me just as well as they'd fit Devon. Despite our different lifestyles, we had stayed a remarkably close match in our physical forms. And of course, as far as features and coloring went, we'd always been shockingly identical. What looked good on my brother would look good on me. But I didn't want it. It was all just another reminder of all the things my family had cared about more than I did—money, prestige, power symbolized by glamor and frivolous excess.

I yanked open another dresser drawer to find set after set of twinkling cufflinks. Gold, silver, some with diamonds, some with engravings. The stuff in the drawer was easily worth more than most people made in an entire year. Hell, it was worth more than some people made in their entire lives. It turned my stomach, to be honest. I slammed the drawer, then raked a hand through my short dark hair. I shouldn't be here. I should be with SEAL Team Four, looking out for the only brothers I had left. I had been in command for a little more than a year after our former CO, Adrian Pierce, abruptly retired. I didn't have time to deal with this mess. I had bigger obligations to things that mattered.

Instead, I was stuck right back into my family's mess, the one place I swore I'd never be again.

I looked around the room with a disgusted sneer. For all the amenities and expensive artwork hanging around the condo, there were no family photos at all. Another Shepperton trait—family came last.

My phone buzzed in my pocket, and I pulled it out to see another text from the head of the company's legal department.

Emergency Meeting Scheduled 9am Tomorrow. Devon's Office.

The knot of tension in my neck tightened further and I cringed, rolling my shoulders to try and loosen the muscles. Dammit. I wanted to go sit in some stuffy financial meeting about as much as I wanted to get a root canal done, but I had no choice. If I didn't show up, I'd leave all the workers for the company in peril. And I was nothing if not a protector. Underdogs, the underprivileged—basically anyone who needed help, I was their guy. I fixed problems.

Too bad there was no one else around to help me fix this mess I was in now.

Frustrated and restless, I tossed my phone on the massive bed in the center of the room and stalked out to the fancy restaurant-grade kitchen to see if my brother had any decent booze in the place. I wasn't much of a drinker, normally, but damn if liquor didn't sound like manna from heaven about now.

I'd just yanked open the door to the large double-sided, stainless-steel fridge and peered inside, when a knock sounded on the front door. I frowned, glancing back over my shoulder. I wasn't expecting anyone and as far as I knew, my brother's address wasn't listed for security reasons. While there had never been any serious threats, apparently it wasn't possible to run a manufacturing company without ticking some people off. That meant that Devon's home address hadn't been widely known, even within his social circle. So who could be at the door? Had some nosy neighbor spotted me coming in and out of the condo and decided to bring over a casserole or something?

I sighed and straightened, bracing myself for painful small talk with a stranger. No, I wasn't Devon, I was Drake… the other half of the Shepperton equation. Yes, Devon and I had been twins. Yes, such a tragedy —so young, etc. Sure, I supposed it was a comfort to know it had happened quickly, without a lot of suffering.

That much was true, at least. Devon had died instantly, according to the coroner. Hell, he'd been dictating a text at the time, from what the police found on the vehicle's black box. Something about money. Figured. Chasing more cash until the end. The Shepperton way. But I probably wouldn't mention that to the neighbor.

Nor would I mention that, personally, I'd rather live on the street than in some palatial prison like this.

Give me a tent in the dusty desert and a war to win, and I was a happy camper.

The knocking sounded again, louder and faster this time.

Damn. I'd hoped they'd go away if I ignored it.

Apparently not. Stalking over to the door with a bottle of locally brewed ale, I turned the handle, bracing myself to be polite.

"I'm so sorry to bother you, but—" The woman in front of me was unfairly pretty: shoulder-length brown hair and pretty pink lips. She was fiddling with her phone, but when she looked up, her doe eyes widened, and what little color was in her cheeks drained away before my eyes. She wavered on her feet. "Oh God. You…it can't be. You're dead… I…"

I grabbed her arm before she toppled over, intrigued despite myself. She looked familiar, but from where? I'd only been in-country for a week, long enough for the funeral, so I hadn't had time to meet any of Devon's friends, let alone a woman as attractive as her.

"Here, sit down," I said, guiding her to the overstuffed leather sofa nearby. "Let me get you some water."

She'd turned an odd grayish color, and I was worried she'd pass out on me.

I rushed to get her water, and then stood, watching, while she sipped at the glass. I hated being caught off-guard…and I disliked even more not knowing why she looked so damn familiar. Was she one of Devon's girlfriends? It was a possibility.

My brother's appetite for wealth had only been rivaled by his lust for the next "new" thing, be it women or cars or luxury yachts. Devon enjoyed sending me pictures of his so-called "glamorous" lifestyle. Maybe she was from one of those pictures—that could explain why I half recognized her.

"Feeling better?" I asked after a moment, glad to see a bit of pink return to her face.

The woman nodded, her gaze still lowered to the glass in her lap. "Yes, thank you. I'm sorry. I didn't mean to act like such an idiot. I was just surprised to see someone who…"

Her voice trailed off again, but I could fill in the blanks.

It wasn't the first time someone had mistaken me for Devon. We were identical, after all, at least on the outside. Same six-foot-plus height, same dark hair and eyes, same muscular build—though mine came from honest hard work while Devon's had been courtesy of some state-of-the-art gym equipment and an expensive personal trainer. Anyway, we got mistaken for each other a lot. Or we used to, anyway.

An odd pinch settled in my heart. Devon and I might have lived very different lives, and we'd had next to nothing in common…but we had still been twins. Despite not liking—or, hell, respecting him very much —the bond that he and I forged in the womb had been unseverable.

At least until now. The strange emptiness that had been lurking around my edges crept a little farther into my soul.

Absently, I took a large swig of the ale, then plopped down into an armchair across from the woman. "It's okay," I said, picking at the label on my bottle. I shrugged, resisting the urge to rub my sore neck again. "Happens a lot. Or used to, anyway. It's been a while since I've been home. I take it Devon didn't mention he had a twin?"

She shook her head. "No. He mentioned that he had a brother, but he rarely talked about you—and I had no idea that you were twins. But then I didn't know him that well. Or I suppose I did, in a way, but…no. He didn't mention it."

"How did you know him?" I asked, curiosity getting the better of me. "You look familiar."

She extended a slim hand toward me. "I'm Layla Bailey. I work for the Shepperton Foundation." I shook her hand briefly, and then she tucked her hair behind her ear and revealed an entire row of small studs lining the shell of her ear. *Huh.* The small hint of a punk aesthetic was not exactly what I was used to seeing on the socialites who usually frequented my brother's bed, let alone the people who worked for the charitable arm of my family's company. "Or I did, anyway. Not sure how that will all go now with Devon gone." She took another swallow of water, then met my gaze at last. "I'm sorry for your loss."

"Thanks." I sat back and took another swig of ale, hoping the liquor would kick in soon and help alleviate the stress scorching through my bloodstream. I'd kill for a nice, numbing buzz right about now. In the meantime, I examined my guest more closely. The woman seemed nice enough, if a bit quiet. Well dressed, in a pricey black pantsuit with diamonds in her earlobes. She was probably some high society heiress, seduced by my brother's charm into volunteering for the company's charity and falling into his bed. I'd seen the type before. They usually didn't stick around long. "So, you volunteer for the charity. That must've been where I've seen you. Press photos and stuff."

"Maybe." She took a deep breath and seemed to gather her flagging confidence, her slim shoulders straightening once more. "But I'm not a volunteer. I'm actually the Executive Director of the Shepperton Foundation. I worked directly under your brother and oversaw most of the community outreach and coordination. I have a Master's in social work and a BA in business administration, so my skill set fit well with the organization."

"I bet it did," I said, narrowing my gaze on her. To be honest, I was kind of surprised by my brother's choice to date this woman. Remembering some of the previous relationships Devon had had—if you wanted to call them that—I had not been impressed with my brother's taste. This woman seemed very different. But then what did I know? I hadn't seen my brother in ages and, truthfully, I'd never been the playboy my brother had been.

In fact, I'd only had one serious relationship so far and that had failed when I'd joined the SEALs. Long-distance never worked out well when it came to love, at least in my experience. Still, I could see why Devon would have been attracted to the woman across from me. She was polished, poised, and well-educated, given her manners and schooling. I always did love a smart woman. Devon, though, would have gone for her because of those beautiful brown eyes of hers and all that silky hair. Not to mention legs for days and the hint of fine breasts beneath that black jacket and white shirt of hers.

Whoa there, cowboy.

I glanced up to find her watching me with a deepening frown. Oops. Yeah. Drinking on an empty stomach probably hadn't been the wisest idea ever. I set the ale aside and cleared my throat, doing my best to get my mind back on the task at hand. "I appreciate the condolences, but I doubt you came all the way out here just to share them in person. So if you don't mind my being blunt, why *are* you here?"

That air of confidence about her evaporated again, and her hand shook slightly as she set her now-empty water on the coffee table. "I, uh… I spoke with an attorney at Shepperton who said I could find you here."

The knots between my shoulder blades squeezed tighter. Was she hoping for some kind of payoff? Even if their relationship had technically been consensual, Devon had still been her boss, and there were bound to be some news outlets that would jump on the story of the abuse of power. Wouldn't be the first time a male Shepperton had been caught in a compromising position and had to buy his way out of it. Lord knew our father had had his share of indiscretions, and Devon did his best to follow in the family tradition.

"I wanted to talk to you in private."

I bet you did.

I did my best to keep my growing disgust from showing on my face and failed miserably, if the way she flinched was any indication. A muscle ticked near my clenched jaw and I took a deep breath to calm my raging pulse. "Go on then. Tell me what you want."

"I don't think Devon's death was an accident," she said, her response so quiet I would have missed it if I hadn't been paying attention.

It took a moment for those words to sink into my brain, but when they did the air left my lungs in one big exhale. Whatever I'd been expecting her to say, it sure as hell hadn't been that. "What?"

"Devon might have been murdered," she said, watching me closely. "I don't have direct proof, but based on the pieces of evidence I have, I think it's possible."

"What evidence could there be?" I scooted forward in my seat, my tone gruffer than I'd intended due to the shock. "The coroner ruled it an accident. They found traces of alcohol in my brother's system and think it was a factor. They know he was speeding. He was also dictating a text on his phone at the time he went off the road, so he was distracted. Seems pretty cut and dried to me. And anyway, why would anyone try to kill him? I know he wasn't everyone's favorite guy, but murder seems extreme."

"I think maybe he was involved in something dangerous. Something that got out of hand. There were things happening at the charity that weren't right." She used her hands a lot as she talked, moving them around and placing them on her stomach periodically. "Part of my job was to keep abreast of how the grant money the foundation received was disbursed, what organizations and causes we supported. Millions of dollars flow through the charity every year. And I noticed that this past year or so, some of the biggest recipients of the foundation's money didn't seem to have any presence at all beyond a bare-bones website. When I first asked Devon about it, he blew me off. Later, when I showed him specific examples, he assured me he'd signed off on all of the disbursements and that they were going to legitimate organizations. Then I got busy with a bunch of new projects Devon dumped on me, and then we started seeing each other outside of work, and I forgot about it. Until the Romanian orphanage."

I inhaled deeply. So yeah. She'd been sleeping with my brother. For some reason, the confirmation of it bothered me more than I cared to admit. Still, donations from the charitable arm of the company to some far-off country did seem a bit odd. I hadn't exactly kept up with the operations of the foundation, but my parents had enjoyed bragging about everything their money had accomplished. They usually went for things closer to home that would create positive press coverage for the company, like local art museums and hospitals. "Romanian orphanage?"

"Yes. It had all the same hallmarks as the early cases, though it was a much larger amount donated than the previous ones, so I'd brought the similarities to Devon—no real press available on the orphanage, only a website, no real mailing address or physical place of business that I was able to track down. It's not uncommon for charities to be duped by phony organizations, so I thought Devon should know about it to protect the foundation's funds and integrity. I called Devon the week before last and talked to him about it, and he said he'd look into it. The next day, he was dead."

"I see." I scrubbed a hand over my face, more exhausted now than I'd been before. I wasn't sure if it was the drink or the grief or the current conversation catching up with me, but whatever it was, I was tired. Tired of dealing with my family's shit. Tired of cleaning up after my brother. Tired of being the only Shepperton who seemed to give a crap about integrity.

"I'm sure this is hard to hear, especially at a time like this, but I thought you should know, since you're taking over the company." She sighed and hugged her arms around herself tighter. "You should also know that I think whoever killed Devon is also after me."

"What?" My gaze flew to hers again and she placed her hands atop her stomach again. That was odd. Either she was sick, or scared I'd strike her—or both. Lord knew I felt like vomiting myself right about now. The fear in her eyes said she was serious about what she'd said, though. This wasn't a conspiracy theory, and she wasn't jumping to conclusions or being overdramatic. She truly thought Devon had gotten mixed up in something that had gotten him killed—and that she was now being targeted by the killers. "Why would someone want to kill you?"

"Because of what I found. I think that's why they killed Devon, and now they want to shut me up too. If my suspicions are correct, they have been using Shepperton Foundation to launder money. I don't know if your brother knew about it or not, but I think that they took him out to keep him from talking. I think they want to do the same to me."

"Then you should go to the police, not to me." I pushed to my feet, needing to move in order to process all this. "They can help you."

"No, they can't," she said. "Or they won't. They told me that until these people, whoever they are, threaten me directly—preferably in writing— or commit actual physical acts of violence against me, there's nothing they can do to help."

"Dammit." I wanted to punch something, namely my brother, for once again getting himself mixed up in another mess. But since that wasn't an option, I slammed one fist into my palm instead. Layla recoiled into the corner of the sofa as if I'd struck her and my anger grew. Not at her, but at whoever had hit her before, because obviously someone had. Reactions like that were learned, through hard experience. It hadn't been Devon, I didn't think, but it was possible. My disgust at my own family grew stronger. "Has anyone actually threatened you—verbally or indirectly?"

"No, not exactly."

"Not exactly?"

"Someone broke into the foundation's headquarters the day after Devon died and went through our files. Nothing was taken, but it was definitely suspicious…and I think someone may be following me."

It did seem suspicious, though I was loath to admit it. The last thing I needed right now was some mystery to solve on behalf of my shady brother. All I wanted was to settle things here and find a replacement CEO for the company so I could get back to my SEAL team. "Well, I don't know what you expect me to do about it. I've got my hands full with settling my brother's estate and putting his affairs in order so I can get back to my life."

I felt bad for the obviously frightened woman, but I honestly didn't know what she wanted from me. I wasn't a criminal investigator. I wasn't even staying on to run the company. If there was something underhanded going on, it wouldn't be up to me to figure it out—it would be the responsibility of whoever ended up taking over Shepperton, Inc.

A moment passed before Layla Bailey stood and stepped closer to me, her hands covering her abdomen again. Something about that made my own stomach drop to my toes this time. Or maybe that was the resigned, flat look in her eyes. Whatever it was, her next words rocked my universe on its axis.

"There's something else you need to know about my situation right now," she said, her words echoing in the quiet room. "I'm pregnant. With Devon's baby."

TWO

LAYLA

Oh boy.

I hadn't meant to blurt it out like that, but he had been looking at me like he was going to toss me out on my butt at any minute and I'd needed him to know, needed someone to know, in case something happened to me and… God, this was all such a mess.

Dizziness overtook me again. I gripped the back of the armchair and forced myself to breathe, nice and slow until the nausea subsided. I hated coming across as weak or fragile, but it was genuinely a struggle to hold myself together right now. I'd been thrown off balance from the moment Drake Shepperton had opened the door—I hadn't been prepared for him to look exactly like Devon. It was like seeing the man's ghost or something. Like I wasn't freaked out enough about everything happening in my life right now.

"Jesus," Drake finally said, his expression as poleaxed as I felt. "Is it money you want?"

Most people would have been insulted by that, but I could understand where he was coming from. He'd grown up with wealth. He was probably used to it being the first thing that people thought of. Instead of lashing out in response, I maintained my calm and lifted my chin. "I'm not a gold-digger, if that's what you're thinking. I don't want anything from you or your family, other than help in figuring out who killed your brother—and who might, in turn, be after me and his child. Once that's done, I'll be out of your life forever."

He gave a derisive snort. "Sure. Right. The fact you're carrying the rightful heir to the Shepperton fortune never entered your mind, huh?"

"No, it didn't." I pressed both hands over my non-existent baby bump again. It was still early days—I wasn't more than eight weeks along, according to my doctor—but I already loved my baby more than life itself, even if the circumstances of my pregnancy weren't the best. My fling with Devon had ended way before I'd even missed a period, let alone had a positive pregnancy test. Then he'd died before I'd had a chance to figure out how to tell him, and now I was on my own to deal with the situation. Not that I would have expected him to help with the baby, but still—at least my baby would have had a father, even if he wasn't very involved. Now, my baby only had me. I'd have to figure out how to do this on my own, just like I'd done everything else in my life since the age of sixteen. "Look, I know this is all a lot to take in, but I'm telling you the truth. About the money and about my baby. If you want me to sign something saying I won't come after the estate, then I'm happy to do so. If you want me to take a paternity test, I will, but I swear I've not been with anyone but Devon for a while now."

Drake gave me some side-eye on that, and I wanted to kick him. Or kick myself for thinking coming here tonight was a good idea. But mainly him. How dare he judge me and assume I was dishonest or greedy when his own family had enough skeletons to fill a square-mile closet.

Of course, if he knew the secrets about my past, he'd be more than justified in looking at me in distrust. But no one knew those anymore, after all the work I'd done to separate myself from who I used to be. I'd changed my name, moved across the country, rebuilt myself from the ground up and damn well *earned* everything I'd gotten for myself since then. All so that no one would ever have the slightest reason to suspect that my parents were some of the most reviled grifters of the last two decades.

I was a different person from the scared kid who'd gone along with my failed-magician dad to his fake seminars on financial freedom while my mom ushered those too-trusting senior citizens in to fill the chairs. They'd run Ponzi schemes that would make Bernie Madoff blush as they stripped people's pensions away. And they'd gotten caught. Mom and Dad had been in prison for fourteen years now and had at least that long to go on their sentences.

Meanwhile, their daughter had made herself over fresh. Layla Bailey, self-made woman. I'd put myself through college, gotten a respectable job at a respectable company where I gave money to people in need rather than draining it away from them. Taking one damn penny that I hadn't earned was the last thing I was willing to do now. And that was why the only thing I needed from Drake Shepperton was his protection, until I had the proof I needed to get law enforcement involved. In the meantime, he could keep his judgment and his millions to himself.

We stared at each other across the span of several feet until Drake finally swore under his breath and turned away, raking his hand through his hair again. He was so similar to Devon in a lot of ways, but also different. Where Devon had always been so polished, never a hair out of place, Drake was rougher, more feral. At least it seemed that way to me, with the way he was always growling and scowling. Or that could have to do with the fact he'd just lost his brother. I wasn't sure, but at this point I'd give him the benefit of the doubt.

"Will you at least help me get to the bottom of these weird donations?" I asked. "Maybe I'm wrong about the rest—maybe Devon's death really was an accident and no one's following me after all." I *wasn't* wrong—but I wasn't going to be able to convince him of that, which meant I was on my own. So be it. I was used to taking care of myself. I could keep doing it a little longer, with his assistance. Hopefully, by then we'd have enough evidence that I could go back to the cops and convince them I had a case. "But the donations are a problem that needs to be resolved. I really think there's something not right there."

He glanced over at me, then shook his head and returned to his seat. I did the same, feeling shaky and out of sorts. Whether it was because of the pregnancy or the situation, I wasn't sure. All I knew was the past few weeks or so had thrown me for a hell of a loop and I just wanted my old, boring life back. The life I'd had pre-Devon.

Too bad it would be at least seven months now before that happened, if not longer.

I sighed and covered my face. Oh, who was I kidding? I'd kissed that life goodbye the second I'd slept with Devon Shepperton, and it wouldn't be coming back anytime soon. It was the bad decision that kept on giving.

With a grunt, Drake stood, grabbed my glass off the table and went to the kitchen. He refilled it, then returned and handed it to me. "Drink that. Looks like you're going to pass out on me."

"I'm fine."

"Do it anyway. Please. I really don't need a pregnant woman face down on my floor."

I wanted to argue, but the fight had gone out of me. I sipped the water, watching him over the rim. He'd been shocked by my announcements, both the suggestion his brother's accident might not have been an accident at all and my pregnancy news. In retrospect, I supposed it was a lot to throw at him all at once. I was a little relieved that he hadn't thrown me out of the house, or just laughed at me and shut the door in my face. His response hadn't exactly been warm, but he'd heard me out, brought me water, shown some concern over my well-being. If the situation had been reversed, I doubted Devon would have been this patient with one of his brother's paramours.

I didn't know much about Drake Shepperton. In the short time I'd been sleeping with Devon, he'd rarely mentioned anything personal, let alone things about his family. He'd mentioned his brother was in the military, a Navy SEAL, but that was about it. Certainly nothing about them being twins, thus my near faceplant on the front porch when he'd answered the door.

He cracked open a bottled water and downed half the contents before meeting my gaze once more. I felt kind of bad for him, actually. I knew firsthand the way it felt when your family let you down, trapping you in a mess that wasn't of your making. And Drake seemed like a decent enough guy, not that I knew him well. But you had to have some kind of moral code to be a SEAL, right?

"So," he said, after a long beat, looking at me over the rim of his bottle, his brown eyes unreadable. "You said someone's been watching you? Have they tried to break into your home like they did the foundation offices?"

"No. Not that I'm aware of. I live in a co-op building with a doorman who screens all visitors. The guards would've mentioned something, I'd think, if some stranger showed up while I wasn't home, asking about my place. And I haven't noticed any signs that things have been moved or searched."

"Do you have a security system at your place, outside the doorman?" His concern was something else at odds with his brother. Despite the few nights we'd spent together, Devon had never once asked about my life when we were apart, let alone my welfare. He'd liked having sex with me, that was about it. Drake's seemingly genuine concern for a woman he'd only just met, coupled with his near-identical appearance to Devon, was unsettling. When I didn't respond, he continued. "If you're on the first floor, it would be easy enough for someone to jimmy a window to get in. Even on the second floor, it's not impossible for someone to scale the wall and enter your place without the guards knowing. I'm a SEAL, I know there are ways to get in just about anywhere without being detected."

Great. Just what I needed. More to worry about. Luckily, that problem was already resolved. "I've actually been staying at a hotel since the night Devon died." At his curious look, I explained, "Like I said, I was scared whoever killed him would come after me next, so I packed a bag and moved into the Hilton downtown."

Drake whistled. "The Hilton? That's not cheap."

"No, but I've felt safe there." I shrugged. "I could find a cheaper motel, but I'd feel just as exposed there as I did at home. I'd hoped that once the police started investigating, I'd feel safe enough to go back to my place. But that hasn't happened, and while I've got a decent amount in my savings, I don't want to end up spending it all on hotel bills. I'll need to go back to my place soon. Or find somewhere else to stay until all of this is over."

He blinked at me a moment then frowned. "Stay here."

"What?" Now it was my turn to be shocked again. "I can't stay here."

"Why not?" He leaned forward, resting his forearms on his knees, his ale bottle dangling from his long, tapered fingers. The recessed lighting overhead highlighted his muscles and sinews, not that I noticed. Nope. Definitely not looking at how buff he was.

Superficially, his physique was the same as Devon—same broad shoulders, toned biceps, firm chest. But something about the impression of his strength was entirely different. Drake had come by his toned physique the honest way, I was sure, whereas Devon had honed his bod through hours at the gym, staring at himself in the mirror. I'd had to go with him once—we'd been in the middle of discussing plans for a fundraiser when he'd said he absolutely had to leave because he had plans with his trainer. Finishing the conversation had meant tagging along. It had not been what I would have called fun.

Drake continued, drawing me back to the present. "I've been clearing this place out to sell it. There's plenty of room and it would be nice to have someone to talk to besides myself. The building is very secure, and the address isn't publicly tied to Devon, much less to you. Besides, even if someone were to follow you and find out where you were staying, with me here, you can be damned sure no one's breaking in. With you being…" he waved a hand over me vaguely. "Well, in your condition, I'd feel better having you where I can keep an eye on you anyway, until this is all settled one way or another."

I'd not expected that invitation, but it made a kind of sense. I'd feel even safer here than I had at the Hilton—and it would certainly be a lot easier on my budget than continuing to stay at the hotel. I had to watch every dime these days, what with the baby coming and now with Devon gone. Who knew what would happen to the foundation? The new CEO could decide to hire someone else in for my position, or dismantle the program altogether. I might be looking for a new job soon enough and with a kid on the way, employers likely would not be as keen to hire me knowing I'd be off on maternity leave in a few months' time.

Drake watched me closely, then exhaled slowly. "I promise not to bother you. Separate bedrooms, separate bathrooms. Given the size of this place, we'd only have to see each other in passing, if that's what you'd prefer. Or if you want more interaction—to feel safe, and to work through this whole mess with my brother and the charity—then I'll be right here whenever you need me. I'll even give you a ride to the hotel."

I took a deep breath and nodded. Given my current circumstances, it really was an offer I couldn't refuse. "Fine. Let's go pack up my things."

THREE

DRAKE

E arly the next morning, I found myself at the last place I'd ever
thought I'd see again: Shepperton, Inc.'s corporate offices. The
building still looked the same as I remembered, still cold and stuffy,
with all its modern décor and bland artwork.

Maggie Thompson, my brother's long-time assistant, sat across the
desk from me, filling me in on the upcoming meetings and public
appearances that were still on Devon's schedule that she hadn't been
able to cancel. For the time being, I would have to step in. I did not
want to be the new head of my family's old company, but there were a
lot of people who depended on Shepperton, Inc. for their livelihoods.
Until I found a suitable buyer, I couldn't do anything that would make
the company look unstable or possibly drive down the share price—not
when I was looking for someone to purchase the operation with, hopefully, as little disruption to the workers as possible. That meant that, as
much as I could, I'd have to try to keep things business as usual—no
matter how it turned my stomach.

"Other than the emergency meeting at nine, your time is free today,
sir," Maggie said, her neatly bobbed silver hair shining in the bright

sunlight streaming in through the windows. She'd joined Shepperton back when my parents had run the company and had seen the executives through good times and bad. Considering I was now the guy in charge, with no clue about running a multi-billion-dollar corporation and no desire to learn, these current times were about as bad as they could get. Still, Maggie's warm smile felt like a little piece of home to me, despite the chill of the place, and I was grateful for her presence. She seemed to feel the same, since she reached across to pat my hand, her blue eyes kind behind her glasses. "I'm glad you're back, sir, even if it is under these terrible circumstances. Your brother could've used some of your no-nonsense good judgment around here."

"Thank you," I smiled back at her, intending to ask her more about Devon's poor judgment in recent months, but the ring of the phone had Maggie back on her feet and heading for her desk, positioned just outside my office, before I could say anything else.

She closed the door behind her, leaving me alone in Devon's old office. My brother's taste in furnishings was the opposite of mine. I liked cozy, comfortable things, stuff that didn't creak under my muscled bulk and accommodated my height and long legs. Drake, on the other hand, apparently preferred style over substance, if the uncomfortable desk chair I sat in was any indication. It shrieked every time I shifted my weight and something in the seat kept poking me in the butt.

Dammit. Restless, I got up to pace the office. Steel and glass shelves lined one wall, but instead of books or personal mementos, the spaces were filled with ridiculous sculptures that probably cost a fortune but looked like a toddler made them. Such a stupid waste of money. All of it. Hell, the sale of even half this crap could probably feed one of the starving villages I'd visited on various missions over the years. The weird, brightly-colored blob on one shelf actually reminded me of the flag of the Republic of Wathaan—but that might have been my mind playing tricks on me. That was the mission where we'd lost Kyle. The mission that was already resting way too damn heavily on my mind as I got closer and closer to the one-year anniversary. *Don't go there,* I reminded myself.

Instead, I looked at the wall of useless junk and sighed, thinking of all the good Devon could have done with his money instead. All the people he could have helped. What a goddamned waste.

My brother's blindness to others' needs turned my stomach, but I couldn't blame Devon for it completely. It was how he'd been raised— how we'd *both* been raised. Devon's callousness was typical of our whole family. In all of my memories, I couldn't remember a time when the Sheppertons had been together, as a family, without all the trappings of wealth and privilege, to just enjoy each other as people. Nope. With my clan, money was always involved. Always.

It was sad. It was pathetic. It was infuriating.

And right now, it was taking every ounce of strength I could muster not to walk out and leave it all behind forever. Forget the emergency meeting. Forget all my brother's shady dealings. Forget everything.

Except I couldn't forget everything. People were depending on me. The workers were depending on me. Layla Bailey was depending on me now too. Layla Bailey and her unborn baby.

I sighed and leaned my shoulder against the wall beside the window to stare out into the blue skies above. At least the clouds were gone. April in Dallas was usually pretty nice, and it looked like it might end up being a sunny day. Perhaps that was a sign things would get better here. Given the crappy situation, I was going to take any hint of hope I could find.

I strode back to the desk, shoved Devon's uncomfortable chair aside and pulled one of the comfier wing guest chairs around behind the desk to sit in. Much better. Then I went through the stack of documents

Maggie had brought in along with my agenda. But as I stared at the numbers and figures and cost projections, my mind kept wandering back to Layla and our conversation the night before.

More specifically, the baby. Devon's baby.

The idea that my brother had gotten a woman pregnant still boggled my mind. While it had been years since we'd lived under the same roof, I knew that Devon had always taken contraception seriously, which was good since he'd slept his way through half the women in Dallas before his twentieth birthday. Still, mistakes happened, and I didn't doubt that Layla was telling the truth about my brother being the father. Looking at the law of averages, it had only been a matter of time, really. Plus, if my brother's judgment had been as compromised recently as everyone seemed to suggest, then that only upped the odds he'd risk unprotected sex.

Taking a deep breath, I switched on the monitor on the desk and typed Layla Bailey's name into the search engine. PR pictures from one of the Shepperton Foundation's charity galas last Christmas popped up. The same photos I had seen before. Layla stood at Devon's side, her smile radiant and her creamy skin glowing against the burgundy satin and lace ball gown she wore. Her beauty struck me once more, the same way it had the previous evening. With her dark hair and large, dark eyes, she was striking. And usually just my type of woman. But I wasn't about to get involved. Not with anyone, and especially not with Layla—anyone who'd been romantically attached to Devon couldn't possibly be a good fit for me. I was only here to clean up my brother's mess and get rid of the family business for good.

And protect my brother's baby...

My stomach clenched at the reminder and my shoulders hunched, causing my neck muscles to seize up again. *Ouch, dammit.* I rubbed a hand over the nape of my neck, but it did little good. Stress had become more and more of a problem for me, ever since I'd taken over as team leader a year ago. I'd been about to see the Navy doctor about some muscle relaxers before I'd gotten the call about Devon and had to scramble to deal with the funeral arrangements while arranging for bereavement leave and my transport home. Maybe I'd go see someone this afternoon, since Maggie had said the rest of my day was free after the emergency board meeting.

Ugh. I returned to my paperwork and did my best to focus. Bad enough I had to act as interim figurehead for the company until I could find someone else to take it over. To walk into that boardroom unprepared would be even worse. But I didn't do things half-measure. It wasn't my nature.

As I studied the balance sheets before me, showing a debit side of things that was much more crowded than the credit side, it seemed nothing had changed in the years since I'd been gone. Even for a non-numbers guy like me, it was obvious that Devon had taken a lot more chances with the company assets in recent years than anyone could possibly consider reasonable. Some had been disasters, a lot had just barely broken even—but a few had been successful enough to keep Devon constantly chasing the next victory. Yes, the company had remained profitable through all of it, but it was a damned stupid, risky way to run a business.

God. What a mess.

I thought again about Layla's claim that Devon had been murdered. Was this the reason why? Had his adrenaline addiction driven him to get involved with things that weren't exactly lawful? I considered looking for answers myself, knowing that if I really dug in, I'd be able to figure everything out. I'd always been good at research, and I'd developed some serious computer skills over the years. It started out as a hobby, but after it paid off in spades on a couple of missions, it became something I worked to develop. I might not be formally trained, but I had always been my team's "tech guy."

But between running the company, wrapping up my brother's estate, and keeping an eye out for Layla in case she was right and someone really *was* after her, I didn't have the time for a deep dive.

Time to call in reinforcements.

I picked up the phone and called Zach Walker. We'd served on the same team for years—but everything changed after we lost Kyle. Our team leader, Adrian, blamed himself for the mission going south, and he vanished on us. No one heard a word from him for months—we were half convinced he was dead—when out of the blue, we found out he was at Quantico, training to join the FBI. I was glad to hear he was doing something with his life…but I had to admit, it hurt that I hadn't heard from him directly in damn near a year. Zach didn't ditch us like that, but after the RoW, it was clear that he'd lost the stomach for the job. When his term ended in November, he decided not to re-up. Now, Zach was a private investigator; he'd set up shop in Dallas.

"Walker Investigation, you've got Zach," he said after two rings.

I smiled so hard, and my face ached. It felt like the first proper smile in weeks. "You don't have a secretary yet, Walker?"

"Shep?" Zach asked. "What the hell are you doing calling me from a stateside number?" I quickly briefed him on what happened to Devon. Zach hissed softly, but thankfully, he didn't offer his condolences. Like me, he knew they were more of a comfort for the person offering them than for the person getting them. "How can I help?"

"His ex, Layla, seems to think that Devon's accident might not have been quite so accidental. Could you look into it for me?"

"Sure thing," Zach said without hesitation, and for a moment, I really,

really missed my team. They felt more like brothers than my own twin did. "I'll send over any questions that I have."

"Thanks, man."

Zach sucked his teeth. "So…you hear from Pierce? Kelley told me he's a Fed now."

Last I'd heard, he was still in training…but thinking back on the timeline, I realized he'd probably just finished his course. "I know," I said, "and no, I haven't spoken to him. He's a ghost, man."

"You should call him. Kelley said he's working on—"

"I know about that too," I cut him off. Adrian was on a one-man mission to prove that there was some big conspiracy behind everything that went wrong in the mission—leading to Kyle's death. "If that's how he wants to grieve, let him, yeah? Maybe it'll help him make sense of it all." Not that there was much sense in death. Look at Devon's accident. My brother was in the prime of his life, on top of the literal world, and he wrapped his expensive car around a tree. Poof. Gone. "Look, I appreciate you helping me out. Send me a list of what you need, and I'll get it to you as soon as possible."

"Sure, sure, man." Before I could hang up, he said, "You said you're in contact with your brother's ex, huh? She pretty? Layla's a pretty girl's name."

Asshole. But even the thought was fond. Death truly did make sentimental fools out of us all. "Shut up, Walker," I groaned and hung up on him before he could say another asinine thing.

Before I could decide what to do next, there was a knock on the door, and Maggie poked her head in again.

"Sorry, sir, but Ms. Bailey's here to see you," the older woman said.

"That's fine," I nodded. "Send her in. Oh, and Maggie?"

"Yes, sir?"

"Please call me Drake. You've known me since I was five. Sir was for my father." I winked.

"Very good then, Drake." Maggie grinned. "I'll send Ms. Bailey in. You have twenty minutes until your meeting."

"Thank you." I stacked the paperwork and shoved it aside as Layla walked in the door, dressed neatly once again, in a gray pantsuit this time, with a dark green blouse underneath. When I'd left Devon's condo earlier this morning, she'd still been in her robe, her hair tousled and tangled as she'd made herself a cup of tea. Seeing her disheveled and barefoot—looking far too much like a woman who'd just exited her lover's bed—had done strange things to me, so I was glad to see Layla all buttoned-up and businesslike again. I watched while she took a seat in the remaining wing chair in front of the desk and set her bag near her feet. "Good morning."

"Morning," she said, meeting my gaze at last. There were shadows beneath her lovely eyes, and I wondered if she'd slept well last night in the guest room. I started to ask, then stopped myself, figuring that might be too personal. We didn't really know each other that well, after all. She tucked her hair behind her ear, revealing all those glittering ear studs again. I wanted to ask her about those too. Tons of piercings weren't exactly what you normally saw on corporate execs. She bent to remove a folder from her bag and her hand shook slightly. I frowned. Was she nervous? Why was she nervous? Surely she wasn't frightened of me. Didn't she know how committed I was to making sure she and the baby stayed safe? That was the whole reason I'd asked her to move in. My mind darted to the next obvious answer. The baby. Was there something wrong with the baby? Had she been ill this morning? What I knew about pregnancy would barely cover the head of a pin, but morning sickness was a thing, wasn't it?

Then Layla laid the folder on the desk in front of me and drew me back to the present. "Here are the financials for the Romanian orphanage donation. I mentioned them last night, but I thought you might want to check them out more in-depth before your meeting this morning."

"Right. Thanks." I frowned down at the folder, doing my best to concentrate on what she was saying and not the spicy sweet scent of her perfume drifting around me now. It was nuts. I didn't usually go around sniffing women's perfume. I was a SEAL, dammit, not some lust-crazed teenager. I shook off the disturbing awareness of her and scowled down at the reports she'd given me. "Tell me again what you've done so far with these."

"Well, first I tried to find any paper trail of them—records of work they'd done, organizations they'd partnered with, other donations they'd received. I couldn't find anything. Not even a photograph of the children or the building. As far as I can tell, there *is* no building—just a post office box. The website gives barely any information at all, and it's very generic. With all of that to back up my suspicions, I questioned Devon about them," she said, clasping her hands in her lap to hide their trembling. "When I first mentioned it to him…"

I gave her a sharp look when she hesitated. "What?"

"Well, he said that it was *your* idea to give them money after being stationed nearby for a while."

I couldn't help my incredulous expression before I quickly schooled my features. Poker face. That was SEAL training 101. Never show your emotions to your opponent. Not that Layla was my opponent. She was… Well, I didn't know what she was at the moment, but we weren't enemies. Still, until I knew what we were dealing with, I wanted to be as calm and dispassionate about this as I could be. I cleared my throat and jabbed the report with my finger. "I can tell you with one-hundred-percent certainty that I never made any recommendations to the foundation concerning this orphanage or anyplace else. I've never had any involvement at all with Shepperton, Inc., or the foundation until now. And I've never set foot in Romania."

"I believe you." Layla gave me a small smile, her tense shoulders relaxing slightly. "It's nice to hear my suspicions confirmed, though. Not that I'm glad to hear something shady happened—but at least I know I haven't been overreacting, seeing problems where there weren't any."

"Hmm." I glanced through the rest of the papers in the folder, then closed it and folded my hands atop it, my tone deadly serious. "I've contacted an associate of mine to look into the details of Devon's accident and to check into his accounts. Given my family's wealth and connections, I'm not sure I trust the local police to catch all the pertinent details, especially since they've already concluded that the crash was nothing more than an accident. This PI is an ex-SEAL and will do a thorough job. If it turns out to not be an accident at all, this investigator is also discreet and will keep it between us until we direct him otherwise."

"Good to know." Layla fussed with the edge of her immaculate jacket. "Did Maggie go over the calendar with you?"

"She did," I said, sitting back. "Not looking forward to any of it and hope to rearrange most of it. Maybe cancel a few things too. My brother did way too much self-promotion. That's not my thing at all. Under the circumstances, I'm sure people will understand."

"They will," she agreed, then leaned forward, stirring the air around me with her scent again. I did my best to ignore it, along with the way her position caused the front of her shirt to gape slightly, allowing me a glimpse of the base of her throat and the creamy expanse of her upper chest. My body tightened despite my wishes and I shifted in my seat. Whatever this strange connection was that I felt with Layla Bailey, I didn't like it. Not at all. She narrowed her gaze on me, then laughed. "Didn't like your brother's chair?"

"No. It was uncomfortable as hell," I said, a bit off kilter at the sudden change of topics.

"I always thought it looked horrible, but Devon was so proud of it—apparently, it's one of a kind, made by a famous designer." She sat back in her seat. "I understand wanting to stick to what makes you comfortable—either in chairs or in public events—but I hope you're not planning to cancel your appearance at the opening ceremony for the children's medical wing of the hospital," she said, knocking me off-balance again. "The Shepperton Foundation made major donations to fund the renovations and they've been planning this grand reopening for months now. It would make a positive statement if you came—showing continuity in our path going forward. Plus, you'd leave me without an escort if you backed out."

"Oh, well." I shifted my weight again, glad to see a bit of colour had returned to her cheeks and that her dark eyes had some sparkle again. If I didn't know better, I'd think she was flirting with me. But that would be impossible, right? We barely knew each other. She was pregnant with my brother's baby. We were trying to solve a mystery together, not hop into bed. It was probably just my stress levels screwing with my perceptions again. My neck gave a twinge as if in agreement. "I don't know. I'm sure you can find a suitable replacement for me. I'm not very good company at parties anyway and—"

"Drake?" Maggie's voice rang over the phone intercom system. "They're ready for you in the board room."

Shit. So much for being prepared.

Layla was still watching me from across the desk, her lovely face a mix of apprehension and hope. "The event's in two days and the PR materials have already been reprinted to list you as attending. I know it won't be a lot of fun for you, but as the acting CEO, it really would mean a lot if you would come. Also, I thought it might give us a chance to ask around and see if Devon might have had strange encounters with any of the other donors present. There should be a number of people there who interacted with him on a regular basis—they might have seen something I didn't."

Man, I hated disappointing people almost as much as I hated socializing. And she did have a point. It might be a good chance to snoop around some more into Devon's dealings. Also, that image of her in the burgundy ball gown kept flashing into my head, and damn if it wouldn't be nice to see her all dressed up like that once before I left town for good. Not that I'd tell her that. A glance at the clock said I was out of time. I stood and waited while she gathered her things, then walked her to the door. "Fine. I'll go with you. But don't expect me to schmooze like my brother did."

"Great." Layla's beaming smile was more than payment enough for the uncomfortable evening I'd have to endure on Wednesday. "It's a date then."

I stood in the doorway long after she'd walked away, wondering what the hell I'd just agreed to and why my blood was fizzing with a mix of adrenaline and excitement at the thought of attending the event with her. We'd be going as colleagues. To fulfill my obligation as the company's CEO and look into my brother's shady dealings. Nothing more. The sooner I remembered that, the better.

FOUR

DRAKE

It was actually good that my schedule was clear after the board meeting because I ended up getting a tour of the accounting department from the department's head, Jameson Peterkin, former CFO of Shepperton, Inc.—at least until Devon had decided to take over that role himself that last year or so.

The fact that my brother had assumed control of the financials for the company only raised my suspicions further. In a company of this size, CEO should have been job enough for anyone. The only reason I could think of as to why Devon would want to pile on the CFO responsibilities too would be if he didn't want anyone else to get a full view of the company's financials. Of course, I didn't mention that to Jameson. Not yet. Not until I had more proof against my brother. For now, I hoped to win the man's trust in order to get more information out of him.

Luckily, the man seemed to be more than willing to talk. And he didn't hesitate to be frank about his opinion of Devon.

"Forgive me for saying so, but your brother wasn't the easiest man to work for," Peterkin said, fiddling with his bowtie. He was an accountant through and through and looked the part. "I have to say that having Devon here, micromanaging every aspect of my department, was unsettling to say the least. Toward the end, I was feeling rather…"

"Harassed?" I filled in the blank for him.

"Quite," Jameson agreed. "It was odd, because your brother hadn't been very hands-on where balance sheets were concerned prior to that. When he took over as CFO and demoted me to head of accounting, I was shocked. But I still tried to provide assistance as needed. I've been with Shepperton since your parents were here and I have a lot of loyalty to this business. I didn't want to overstep my bounds, mind you. Just looking out for the company. This place is like family to me."

I wished I could say the same. But then, I didn't like the company and I didn't like my family…so maybe it *was* like family to me, in the worst way possible.

I nodded to the man and patted him on the back. "Well, I'm here now to straighten out this mess as best I can. I wonder if you could provide me with the financial reports for the past two quarters?" When Jameson balked a bit, I added, "I just want to make sure I have the full picture of where we stand, so I know where the company needs to go from here. Can't say I'm exactly a numbers guy, but I should be able to at least make heads and tails out of it."

"Oh, well." Jameson fiddled with his bowtie again, then adjusted his glasses. "Of course, sir. It's just that it might take me a few days to get it all together. That's a lot of data."

"Don't worry about it. I'm sure you have plenty of other responsibilities, and I don't want this to impede the rest of your work. A few days is fine. Neither of us is going anywhere for a while, right?" I gave the nervous man what I hoped was a reassuring smile, despite the tension roiling inside me. Devon had definitely been up to some hinky shit before he died, there was no doubt in my mind about it now. I just hoped it wasn't so horrible that I couldn't repair the damage done—and that it wouldn't take forever to get the company back on the right track again so I could pass it over to someone else and get back to my real life. "Just send it through Maggie once you get it ready, okay?"

"Yes, sir," Jameson said, holding out his hand. "Thank you, sir."

"Please, call me Drake," I said, shaking the man's hand. "And as of now, you're CFO again."

"Thank you, si—" Jameson stopped himself. "I mean Drake. Thank you."

"My pleasure." I exited the accounting department, my long strides eating up the distance to Devon's office in record time. It was after four now, and my head was near to bursting with all the new information I'd learned about Shepperton, Inc., the charity foundation, and my brother's destructive leadership of the company. If Devon had been there, I'd have punched him in the face. As it was, I needed time and space to process everything before I decided how to move forward.

After gathering a few things from the office, I bid Maggie goodnight and headed back to the condo. Layla was there when I arrived, working on her laptop at the dining room table.

"How'd the board meeting go?" she asked as I passed by on my way to the kitchen for a drink.

"It was interesting. Even more interesting was my tour of the accounting department afterward."

"Really?" Layla closed her laptop and looked over at me expectantly. "Did you find out more about Devon's activities?"

"Not yet, but I wasn't happy to learn he'd named himself CFO last year." I twisted the cap off of my bottle of ale and took a huge swig before continuing. "The whole reason for having the CEO and CFO positions separate is to create checks and balances. Merging the two together only makes him look more suspicious."

"Agreed." Layla sighed. "When that happened, I didn't know Devon well enough to say anything to him about it. Then, after we started sleeping together, it seemed awkward to bring it up, especially with the whole donation thing going on, so I didn't." She shook her head. "Maybe I should've said something to him back then. Maybe that would've stopped all this before it started."

"I doubt he would've listened to you," I said, tossing the cap in the recycle bin, then joining her at the dining room table. "My brother wasn't exactly open to other people's opinions. He always assumed he knew best—and that he could get away with anything if he set his mind to it. He used that credo to justify a lot of horrible behavior. From what the other employees I've talked to have said, he was basically an ass to everyone he considered beneath him." Once the words were out, I regretted them, especially when I caught Layla's wince. "Sorry. I'm sure he was different with you."

She hung her head, the silky fall of her hair obscuring her face again. My fingertips itched to push the strands away, to see if her hair felt as soft as it looked. I barely managed to tamp those crazy urges down. Layla wasn't mine to touch. She was here because she had nowhere else safe to go and because we were working to find out the truth about Devon. That was it. She shrugged and raised her gaze to meet mine. "I wish I could say that was accurate, but it's not. He was mostly an ass to me too, except when we were having sex."

I took that in for a minute, working hard to suppress the odd rush of anger and envy that rushed through me along with the unwanted image of my brother and this lovely woman in bed together. Devon hadn't deserved someone like Layla, no matter how much money and power he'd had. But their relationship also raised the question of why she'd chosen to be with my brother in the first place. I wanted to ask but didn't feel comfortable doing so at that point.

Instead, I stood and headed down the hall to my bedroom. "Be back. Need to shower and change."

An hour later, I emerged again, clean and relaxed, though my head was still swimming with the information I'd learned that day. Layla was back to working on her computer and I needed something to distract myself, so I padded into the kitchen barefoot and checked the fridge. I'd called the store earlier and had them deliver groceries. I supposed I could just make a sandwich for dinner, but I felt like putting in a bit more effort—especially if I wasn't going to be cooking just for one.

"Are you hungry?" I called over to Layla, who was typing away on her keyboard. "It's after six. You should eat something."

She looked back at me, her face ghostly pale in the light from her screen. "Okay. I can make something."

"No, no. You sit. I'll cook dinner." I chuckled at her dubious expression. "Seriously. I like to cook, and I'm pretty good at it. I promise I won't poison you. You like chicken and pasta?"

"I do," she said after a moment.

"Great. Finish up whatever you're working on because I'll knock your socks off with my alfredo recipe."

Layla's laugh seemed to brighten the darkening room a bit and I turned away fast so she wouldn't see how happy her response made me. My reaction to her was crazy enough as it was.

Thirty minutes later, I served up two heaping bowls of creamy, cheesy pasta and chicken and she closed down and put away her laptop. We dug into our food while the TV murmured low in the background and sparkling water bubbled in our glasses.

"Wow, this is amazing," she said after devouring another large bite of pasta. "Where'd you learn to cook like this?"

"Thanks. And this particular recipe I learned after I lost a bet in college. The terms of the bet meant that I had to learn to make thirteen different dishes, actually, though this one was my favorite. Afterward, I kept cooking because I loved it so much. I've picked up lots of recipes from around the world."

"I bet." She sipped her water and watched me over the rim. "I'm envious. I can't really cook at all. Or at least, I don't think I can. I don't usually bother trying. Not so much fun when you're only making food for one."

I swallowed another bite of chicken, taking in her response before asking, "What about your family? Don't you have anyone close by? Parents? Siblings? Cousins?"

"No." She took a deep breath. "No one really. There's my grandmother, but I don't like to bother her. It's complicated."

"Right." I smiled over at her, hoping to lighten the somber mood that had fallen over us. "Well, if anyone understands family drama and complications, it's me."

We ate in silence for several minutes. Layla kept her gaze lowered to her plate, and I tried to think of something to say that would get her talking and smiling again. I didn't like to think I'd upset her, especially since she'd opened up to me a bit about her family situation. Maybe some assurances would help, since she had to be worrying about her future with the baby coming and all, right? Especially since it sounded like she'd be on her own, since the baby's daddy was gone and Layla didn't have any family to fill the gap. "So, once Devon's estate is settled and this mess is cleared up with the foundation, I want you to know that I'll make sure you and the baby are well taken care of. You won't have to worry about your job or your living arrangements. I'll make sure it's all settled before I go back to my SEAL team. It's the least I can do after how my brother handled things."

Layla blinked at me, silent, and my heart nosedived again. Did I screw up? The look in her brown eyes was unreadable, so I had no clue how to read her reaction. Finally, she exhaled slowly and shook her head. "Don't worry about it. I doubt Devon would've welcomed our baby, so I planned to handle things myself anyway. It's not like we were in love or anything, so I don't really feel comfortable taking anything from you or the company."

Once more those questions swirled in my mind about how she'd ever ended up involved with my brother. Though I had to admit that a tiny part of me was glad to hear that there'd been no emotional involvement between them and that it had only been a fling, nothing serious. I wasn't ready to admit why I felt that way, not yet, but it was better knowing it had only been sex. Honestly, I could understand why she might have chosen a relationship like that, given I'd only had one long-term relationship in my life back in college, and we'd broken up when I'd joined the Navy. In the years since then, I'd grown used to short affairs. No fuss. No muss. No strings attached.

The fact that that sounded an awful lot like my brother's style caused that damned twinge in my neck again and I reached up to massage the sore area with my hand.

"Strain?" Layla asked, watching me again.

"Huh?" I frowned. "Oh, you mean my neck. Nah. Just stress. It's nothing important. I'll take some pain meds and be fine."

"If you say so." She finished her last bite of chicken and pushed away her empty plate. "Thank you for dinner. It was excellent."

"You're welcome." I stopped her when she started to clear her dishes away. "Nope. I got those too. You relax and enjoy your evening. I insist."

"Oh." Her gorgeous smile returned, and I felt like I'd just won the lottery. "If you're sure, then I've been dying to try out that jacuzzi tub in Devon's master bath."

"Have at it," I said, standing to take my plate to the kitchen. "I think there's some special bath stuff under the sink. I wasn't sure what to do with it, so I left it there for now. Use it up if you want."

"Thanks. I will." She started down the hall and I did my best not to watch her leave.

Alone, I rinsed the plates and put them in the dishwasher, then set the pans to soak in the sink, my mind whirling with thoughts of Layla and how I needed to keep my head on straight where she was concerned. She was the first woman who'd piqued my interest in a while, but she wasn't a toy to play with. Given her situation and mine, it was best not to even go down that road with her, no matter how attracted to her I was. I'd be gone as soon as the estate was settled, and she had a baby on the way. I wasn't looking for anything long-term and she had commitment written all over her.

At most I could offer her an affair, and she deserved so much more than that.

I finished up in the kitchen, then slumped down on the sofa in the living room to watch TV. I wasn't my brother. Devon was selfish and self-centered, thinking only about his own wants and needs. I refused to be that guy, especially where Layla was concerned. So I'd keep my desires to myself and stick to my plan—no touching, no sex, no attachment. Regardless of how much harder that was becoming the more time I spent with Layla.

FIVE

LAYLA

I arrived early to the opening of the children's wing of the local
hospital, hoping for a chance to mingle with the other attendees and
perhaps build more goodwill for the foundation. I'd had meetings all
day and had barely had time to stop at the condo to change before
coming here, let alone wait on Drake—who seemed completely
uncaring if he was late or not.

Another difference between him and his brother.

Devon used to demand attention wherever he went. Literally. He scheduled his arrivals early and made sure the press knew where he'd be,
which sides gave photographers his best angles, and when to glad-hand
to make the most impact with his high-dollar clients.

There was a slight murmur of voices and a buzz of electric energy
through the crowd. I glanced over to see Drake standing in the doorway, commanding the gaze of everyone in the room without even
trying. He really was something. So similar in looks to his twin brother,
but so different in so many other ways that I was only now discovering.

Before I could stop it, a tiny frisson of attraction blossomed inside me. I tamped it down fast. Yes, he looked exactly like Devon. Yes, Devon and I had slept together. No, that didn't mean Drake and I would share the same sizzling sexual chemistry I'd had with his twin. It was wrong to even think such things. Drake was helping me out of a difficult situation, protecting me when no one else would, sharing his late brother's accommodations with me until I could find other safe shelter. Nothing more. I was indebted to him for his help. It made no sense to complicate things with a pointless crush.

I stepped forward as he crossed the room to me, his tall, muscled physique shown off to perfection in the dark suit he'd worn. Once more my attraction to him spiked before I tamped it down hard. Must be the pregnancy hormones. Yep. That had to be it.

I shook his hand when he arrived, not missing the glint of amusement in his brown eyes. Sure, the greeting was a bit formal considering our living arrangements, but no one needed to know about those. The last thing I needed right now was rumors swirling about me and Drake, not with the offices abuzz over Devon's death. People were already looking a bit askance at me here and I kept resisting the urge to place my hand on my non-existent baby bump for fear I'd confirm what they might be thinking. After all, Devon hadn't exactly been the most discreet person when it came to his romantic affairs and the press had photographed us numerous times at events behaving far more intimately than just boss and employee. If the company knew I was pregnant with his baby, that could put me and my unborn child in far more danger than I was already in.

"You're looking lovely this evening, Ms. Bailey," Drake said, releasing my hand then giving me a quick once-over. "Looks like there's a good turnout."

"Yes. And thank you." I smoothed a hand down the front of my simple black dress. "You look nice yourself. Is that one of Devon's suits?"

He nodded and leaned slightly closer. His warmth and scent surrounded me, musk and cloves and soap. I stared down at the toes of my black pumps and did my best not to picture him in that huge glass and tile walk-in shower in Devon's master suite, water glistening on Drake's arms and chest, trickling lower down his long legs and taut butt, over his…

Oh boy. Yeah, I was in trouble here.

I needed to get it together. Fast.

Thankfully, the MC for the event called everyone to order and the ceremony began with a speech from the Dallas mayor. This was followed in short order by them calling Drake up to the stage to give a brief word to the crowd. I'd warned him earlier that might happen and prayed he didn't freeze up when speaking in public. He always seemed confident, but you never knew what people did when the spotlight turned on them.

Drake gave me a quick wink, then headed for the stage, smiling and shaking hands with various people along the way as if he'd been born to do this, which I supposed he probably had. Yes, he'd left this life behind—but he'd still grown up with it, just as Devon had. Seeing him handle the crowd and the dignitaries on stage made my womb give a traitorous quiver. If I wasn't pregnant already, I was pretty sure his gorgeous, gracious smile from behind that podium would've done the trick.

Dammit, my brain whispered. *Mind in the game, girlfriend. Eyes above the belt.*

I shook off the unwanted thoughts of pinning Drake to the wall and ravishing him silly. What the hell was wrong with me? Fling with Devon aside, I didn't sleep with men casually. Honestly, I didn't sleep with anyone much at all. Up until the affair with Devon, I'd only had one serious boyfriend back when I'd been in college, and that had ended when we'd gone our separate ways after graduation. Since then

I'd been too busy building my career to worry much about relation-ships. In fact, the only reason I'd even started up an affair with Devon was because we were constantly thrown together during events for the organizations sponsored by the Shepperton Foundation, and I'd been bowled over by his determined charm and wicked grin.

Speaking of wicked grins, Drake was beaming down at me from the stage and damn if my blood didn't spark with awareness. His deep voice held me captive as it did everyone else in the crowd, apparently, given that all of them were hanging on his every word. Man, if there was such a thing as star-power, Drake Shepperton had it, whether he knew it or wanted it or not. If he was this good behind a mic, I couldn't imagine how amazing he must be on the battlefield, commanding his SEAL team and achieving one top-secret objective after another.

Drake spoke with surprising insight about the new children's wing and the donors who'd made it possible. I was impressed. I'd been worried whether he'd had time to go over the brief I'd given him earlier, what with all the things he was trying to sort out at the company after Devon's death, but from his speech, Drake had not only read the brief, he'd memorized it. Even more astonishing, he was relaying the infor-mation back now in a friendly, approachable, easygoing manner, not sounding robotic at all, and never doing more than glancing at his note-cards. If I didn't know better, I'd think he'd been part of the company all along, and not off in some far-off location, estranged from the busi-ness and his family.

"And in conclusion, I need to give thanks. First to everyone here for all of your condolences and well-wishes regarding my brother Devon's unexpected passing," Drake said, just the right touch of grief and sincerity in his tone. "Your support during this difficult time means more than I can say and I appreciate everyone who's taken the time to say something to me. I won't forget it." He scanned the crowd before meeting my gaze again. "Finally, I'd like to thank the woman without whose efforts and dedication this ceremony would not have been possible. Let's give a round of applause to the fabulous Executive Director of the Shepperton Foundation, Ms. Layla Bailey."

Heat prickled my cheeks and I smiled, giving nods and thanks to the crowd cheering for me. It was nice. And again, very different from what I was used to with Devon. While he paid me handsomely for my work, he'd never once, as far as I could remember anyway, thanked me publicly for my contributions. Devon always preferred to keep the spotlight on himself.

After Drake and the mayor, along with the hospital's board of directors, stood for yet more pictures, he finally returned to my side. For the first time since his arrival, his broad shoulders hunched slightly and there were lines of tension near the corners of his mouth.

"How long do we have to stay here?" Drake asked me under his breath.

I finished my small glass of punch and set it aside. "We can leave now, if you need to."

"Good." He reached down and took my hand before heading toward the exit. "Let's go."

We said our goodbyes to the crowd as we went, then headed outside to the parking lot.

"Is your car here?" Drake asked, squinting in the sunlight. "I had the company driver bring me over. No sense bothering the guy to pick me up if we can ride back to the condo together."

"Uh, yes." I fished my keys out of my bag and started toward a row of vehicles to the right. "Over here."

But I no more than reached the front of the car when I stopped short.

Based on the lopsided slant to the burgundy SUV, something was very wrong.

"What is it?" Drake said, coming up next to me then cursing under his breath as he took in the sight. "Someone slashed the tires. Call the police."

Crap. There was a slight possibility this was coincidence, I supposed, but a glance around showed me that my vehicle was the only that had been touched. Did that make this a targeted attack? My pulse sped at the thought. Was this related to what had happened at my apartment? Did it have to do with the information I'd found out about the foundation funds or was I being paranoid? Hard to tell anymore. I pulled out my phone instinctively to call the police, then halted. "No. It won't do any good."

"It might." He scowled down at the shredded rubber treads. "And you'll have a report on file as proof for next time. The paper trail of intent has to start somewhere."

"Seems pointless." I sighed. "I mean, they gathered evidence from the break-ins, but they weren't able to find any good leads, so they had to let the investigations drop. And when I tried to say that the crimes showed a pattern of behavior that meant that I was in danger, they argued that they couldn't offer any protection because there was no credible threat of violence against me. Why would a couple of flat tires change anything? They'll just say it was a prank or random vandalism."

"Maybe." He pulled out his own phone to snap pictures of the damage. "But I still think it's a good idea to play this by the book. Anyway, your insurance company might require you to make a police report. Make the call, Layla."

I sighed and did as he asked, then waited twenty minutes until a squad car arrived to take my statement. Sure enough, the officers looked openly skeptical at my suggestion that this was tied to the break-ins or a direct threat to me. They mentioned several other reports of kids vandalizing cars in the area. It was spring break, after all, and teenagers got bored, they said. No, they didn't think it was strange that only my vehicle was attacked. They gave me a police report number and called a tow truck, then left again, leaving me and Drake standing around to find our own way back to the condo. The only blessing was that the sun was setting, easing off some of the heat of the day.

By the time we used a car service to get home, I was hot and tired and more than just a bit cranky.

"C'mon and get changed," he said, slipping off his suit jacket and loosening his tie, making him look far more attractive than a man had a right to be. "I'll make you some tea and then we'll pull up the police report."

I bristled a little at him taking charge and telling me what to do—but the truth was, my feet hurt, and my ankles were swollen, and I had to pee. Again. I wasn't even that far along and already my body was betraying me. Using the bathroom, getting changed, and having some tea sounded like a pretty great idea right now, even if he was the one who'd said it first. Frowning, I toed off my pumps, then headed down the hall to the guest room where I was staying. For some reason, having my tires slashed was just the last straw today. How the hell was I supposed to get to work now? I supposed my insurance company would arrange for me to have a loaner until the car was fixed, but I could already foresee the miserable hour I'd have to spend on hold with the insurance company before that could be sorted out.

Ugh. Tears stung the backs of my eyes before I blinked them away. Must be the pregnancy hormones again. I wasn't normally such a wimp. I was a survivor, dammit. I didn't give up or give in just because one little thing went wrong. If there was any advantage at all to growing up with thieves for parents it was that I learned to be adaptable. Staying on my toes all the time, always ready to run at the first sign of trouble, meant I had to think on my feet.

But working at Shepperton Foundation had given me roots at last, and I hated being forced to resort to tricks from my old life again. Especially since the danger this time didn't come from me being in the wrong, but from me trying to do the right thing where the donations were concerned. And yes, tire damage was small potatoes considering what might have happened to me or my property, but it was still an attack. It was still meant to make me afraid, to restrict my freedom. And for a gal whose parents were in prison, serving long sentences, freedom was a rare and precious thing, never to be taken lightly or lost.

After a quick trip to the bathroom to use the toilet and wash off my makeup, I shed my dress and slipped on a comfy pair of yoga pants and a T-shirt, then slouched back out to where Drake was sitting on the sofa in the living room, a tray with two mugs of tea and a plate of cookies on the coffee table in front of him. The scent of herbs and peppermint tickled my nose as I snuggled into one corner of the sofa, a warm mug clutched in my hands. I was acting like a grump, and hormones or not, there was no excuse for it. Not when he was being so kind to me. "Thank you."

"You're welcome." He picked up his own mug, then placed the plate of cookies between us. "Help yourself. You look a bit pale. I'm guessing your blood sugar's low. You'll feel better if you eat something."

I grabbed an iced gingerbread man from the plate and nibbled on his head. "These are good. Where'd they come from?"

"One of the gifts sent over after Devon's funeral," he said, devouring one of the cookies in three bites. "We need to eat them up before they go stale."

"I don't think that'll be a problem." I grabbed another cookie and chuckled. "These are yummy."

"They are good, right?" He finished off another cookie, then sipped his tea, watching me over the rim. I had no idea where he put all the food, since there wasn't a spare ounce of fat on him that I could see. Just miles of legs and muscle and sinew and…

Whoops.

"If you're worried about your car insurance going up after this, don't. This happened on company time, at a company-sponsored event. I'll make sure the car repair shop sends the bill directly to accounts payable," he said after a moment.

"I'm more worried about how I'll get to and from work until I get my SUV back." I brushed away a few crumbs from the front of my shirt, then sat back into the corner of the sofa again. "My insurance company will probably get me a loaner, but it might take some time to get it all organized. It's a real pain."

"I've got you covered there too." Drake smiled. "No reason why we can't ride to and from work together, right?"

"Are you sure?" I scrunched my nose at him. "I don't want to get in your way or anything. And I know Devon's schedule could be quite unpredictable."

"I'm not Devon," Drake reminded me again, a shadow of something flickering through his dark eyes, there and gone so fast I didn't catch it. "Please? I insist. Plus, it will help me protect you until we catch whoever's doing these things."

I took a deep breath and hesitated. I wasn't used to accepting help from others. I'd been on my own so long, I'd forgotten what it was like to have support—and a part of me was wary of trusting it. But Drake had been nothing but helpful since I'd shown up on his doorstep, whether he wanted to be or not. There was also the fact that he was right. Whoever was behind the break-ins and now my slashed tires was still out there, watching me, waiting. A chill went through me, and I finally gave in to my urge and placed one hand over my abdomen. Funny, but for the first time since all this mess started, I felt safe. Because of Drake.

"Okay," I said at last. "We can ride together. But I will pay you back for all this. I promise."

SIX
DRAKE

The next morning, I was back in the offices of Shepperton, Inc., wading through yet another stack of paperwork and trying to make sense of it all. One of the reasons I'd joined the Navy, other than to get away from my family, was the fact I didn't want to be stuck in some cubicle somewhere, shuffling files for a living. Computers were a *hobby* of mine. Every now and then, I needed to put my skills to work in the field, but I didn't want to be forced to stare at them all day. Being here now made my skin feel itchy. Like I need to get out a run or something.

I'd just finished going over yet another marketing report when the phone on my desk buzzed. I jabbed the flashing red button and picked up the receiver. "Drake Shepperton."

"Mr. Shepperton, this is Jameson Peterkin. Those financial reports you requested are ready. I've sent them to your secure email address."

Great. More numbers. Well, at least these would hopefully shed some light on what the hell my brother had been up to here before his accident. I loosened my tie, hating the damned thing. Felt more like a noose than neckwear. "Thank you."

"You're very welcome, Mr. Shepperton."

"Drake."

"Drake," Jameson corrected, then cleared his throat. "And please let me know if you need anything else from my department."

After the call ended, I pulled up the reports, running a quick query for the red flags Layla had brought up, especially the donations for the Romanian orphanage. Sure enough, Devon had always been the person signing off on those transactions and approving them personally. The contrast was stark, considering that he seemed almost entirely hands-off in most of the foundation's activities, aside from a cluster of donations —both incoming and outgoing—that had his fingerprints all over them from start to finish. Dammit. I sighed and sat back in my seat, rubbing my fingers across my mouth. Devon either knew what was going on or he was a gullible idiot.

I snorted. No. My brother was about as cunning as a fox when it came to business. No way did he not know about the dirty money being cleaned through the charity. The only question was, whose money was being laundered?

A couple more clicks through the reports showed no other interests, financial or otherwise, tied to Devon outside of Shepperton, Inc., so it had to be an outside entity. But that didn't make sense. Why would my brother put the family's considerable interests at risk to clean up someone else's mess? It couldn't have been for the cash. At the time of his death, Devon had been worth billions, as was the company.

One more mystery to solve. One more time suck I didn't need.

Grumbling, I sat forward again and did another query, this time for all disbursement transactions approved by Layla. This time I sorted them by highest to lowest amounts. The biggest donations were in the ten-thousand-dollar range—markedly less than the transactions my brother had green-lighted. In the past two quarters, there had been seventeen of them, all for specific causes—some of them actually for organizations the foundation had been supporting for a number of years, since long before Layla joined the foundation. The rest of the monies spent were spent on general overhead. I opened up another window and did a quick Internet search for the recipient names and found they all checked out. Relieved, I released my pent-up breath. Not that I'd really suspected her of wrongdoing, but given the topsy-turvy situation we were currently in, it was nice to be able to rule that possibility out unequivocally.

I spent the rest of the day going over the rest of the reports Jameson had sent over, then finally stopped around five-thirty. Neck stiff and shoulders knotted, I stood and stretched, removing my stupid tie completely and tossing it down on the desk. Familiar pain shot up the side of my neck and I winced, rubbing the sore area. I needed to take a muscle relaxer when I got back to the condo. Staring at the mounds of paperwork still left for me to go through, I gave a resigned sigh. There wasn't much more I could do by myself. I needed Layla to look at this information too and confirm for me who was and wasn't authorized to sign off on the foundation's grants.

By the time I stopped to pick up Layla from her office and ran a few errands, it was well after six by the time we got home. Layla set her bag on the sofa, then excused herself to shower and change while I shed my business attire for jeans and a sweatshirt before starting some dinner for us in the kitchen—roasted chicken and veggies, along with a salad and some store-bought rolls. The cooking helped me decompress after the stress of the day, though my neck and upper back were still bothering me. I set out one of my pain pills on the counter to take before bedtime. They made me sleepy, and I wasn't ready to zone out yet for the night.

Half an hour later, Layla emerged down the hall, her damp hair slicked back away from her face and a fluffy pink robe tied tight around her over her white and blue pajamas. White socks on her feet completed the look. A far cry from the polished professional I'd picked up from the office earlier. Not that I minded. Honestly, she looked adorable no matter what she wore. Dressed to the nines and styled to perfection. Funny, but when I'd first met her and learned that she'd had an affair with my brother, I'd imagined she was just another one of my brother's socialite bimbos. But now, having spent time with Layla, I knew that wasn't the case. Her clothes were well made, yes, but also practical and professional. Not worn just for fashion, but also for function.

At my curious look, she shrugged. "Sorry, but I wanted to be comfortable. Long day."

"No problem." I smiled, then turned back to the oven to check the chicken while she moved in beside me to get a glass of water from the sink. I hazarded a side glance at her and noticed the multiple piercings in her right ear again. A rainbow of colors sparkled back at me— diamond, emerald, sapphire, ruby, and topaz. Then she turned and I was surprised to find only one earring in her left earlobe, a pink-hued gem I couldn't identify. Curiosity got the better of me and I couldn't help asking, "Tell me about those."

"About what?" She frowned over at me.

"Your earrings." I stirred the veggies on the roasting pan and closed the oven once more, placing the spatula in its holder on the counter. The air smelled of garlic and herbs and warm bread from the rolls also heating in the oven. My stomach rumbled. I'd skipped lunch working on those damned reports about Devon's financial shenanigans. Pain pinched the side of my neck again and I rubbed the sore spot before asking. "I noticed them that first night but didn't say anything. Why so many? And why only on one side?"

She narrowed her gaze on me, her eyes tracking my movement and her expression unreadable. "Have you got a problem with my piercings?"

"No." I held up my hands in the universal sign of surrender, taking a step back. "No problem at all. Just wondered. If you don't want to tell me, though, that's fine. Trying to make conversation."

"Hmm. I'm sorry too, for snapping at you like that. I guess I'm crankier than I thought after today. Or maybe it's my blood sugar again." She sipped her water, then exhaled slowly, her shoulders slumping slightly. Her stomach growled too, and she placed her hand over it, then gave me a small smile. "I got my ears pierced when I was eighteen. It was a...rough time for me. Things had happened in my personal life that made me want to rebel."

I wanted to ask more about that but noticed the shadows crossing her lovely face. Whatever had happened when she was eighteen obviously hadn't been pleasant. If she didn't like to think back on it, then I wouldn't force her to. She'd been through so much, I didn't want to cause her any more upset, so I asked, "Does the right ear have significance? Is there a special reason you got five in that one instead of the other?"

"No. I wish there were a reason—some kind of purpose or message, beyond my own youthful stupidity." Layla chuckled, the sound washing over me like a balm, releasing the knots of tension between my shoulder blades. "And the only significance is as a warning. Whatever you do, kids, never get both ears pierced five times at once." My eyes widened slightly at that, and she grinned. "Yeah, it was a bad as it sounds. I couldn't sleep for three days because of the soreness afterward. Then the left ones got infected, so I took the studs out on that side to treat the infection and so I could sleep again. By the time the infection cleared the holes had healed over already and I was too chicken to go back and get them redone." She smiled wistfully, then reached up and traced her fingers over the glittering stones lining the shell of her right ear. "Besides, I kind of dig the look of having only one ear completely bedazzled, so I stuck with it. Plus, it's a nice ice-breaker conversation-wise, right?"

"Right," I said, my gaze still focused on her right ear. I had the crazy urge to follow the same path with my own fingers…but fisted both hands at my sides to keep from reaching for her. I had no business touching Layla Bailey. Not tonight. Not ever.

Thankfully, the oven timer dinged, distracting me. I slid on an oven mitt to pull out the roasting pan and rolls, then busied myself tossing our salad and putting the warm bread in a basket. Layla helped by putting out the salad and breadbasket while I gathered our plates, silverware, and napkins.

"Accounting sent over some financial reports I'd requested today," I said as I worked, going over my day with her like an old married couple. We'd only known each other a few days, but it seemed so easy to talk to her. I didn't want to think too hard about why that was, so I just went with it. This time with her was the most relaxing part of my day and I didn't want to ruin it. "I spent the afternoon going over them. All those red flags you pointed out are there, plain as day. From what I saw, it's hard not to believe Devon was an active, informed part of it."

Layla stared down at her stockinged toes, frowning. "I'm sorry you're having to deal with all of this after his death. Things must be hard enough for you without learning all these awful things about your brother. If it's any consolation, it was hard for me to believe in Devon's involvement too when I first saw the discrepancies. I thought there must be some mistake, or something I was misunderstanding. That's why I went straight to him with my concerns. But after going over everything, it was the only conclusion I could come up with too. By the time of the accident, he had me questioning everything. I even wondered if he just slept with me to distract me. I don't like to think of myself as a gullible person, but…"

"No. I mean, I can't speak for my brother's motivations in your relationship, nor would I try. Like I said, we weren't close. But I wouldn't blame yourself," I said, setting out our dinnerware on the table, then returning to the counter to dish up our dinner. "And I can't say I'm shocked by Devon's behavior. He was always a ruthless son of a bitch. It's one of the main reasons we never got along. But I am still having a hard time understanding why he'd put the whole company at risk that way."

If she was bothered by me insulting her ex-lover, Layla didn't show it. Instead, she took a seat at the table and nibbled on a roll from the basket I'd placed there. "I've no idea."

After dishing up the chicken and veggies onto a platter, I set it on the table along with a bottle of ale for myself and more water for Layla, then took the chair across from her. "Once we finish eating, I was hoping to have you go over the reports too, if you don't mind. I brought my laptop home with me from the office; I'll hook it up to my system so that we can both look at it." I gestured to my set up in the living room: the only thing of my own I'd bothered setting up since moving into Devon's apartment. I'd gotten myself a pair of monitors and hooked it up to the heavy-duty laptop that I took with me everywhere.

"Sure, whatever you need." She dug into her meal and moaned. "Man, this is great. Thanks for cooking."

"Like I said, I enjoy it." I grinned and twisted the cap off my bottle. "Thanks for eating it."

As we continued eating, I studied her from across the table. She'd mentioned having a rough day and I could see the strain of it in her face. Shadows marred the delicate skin beneath her eyes, and her complexion looked paler than normal. Concern clawed up inside me and I wondered if she was taking on more than she should. After all, Devon's death had to have been a major shock to her, as it had been for me. Plus, she had the pregnancy to contend with on top of it, and the fear of another attack like the one on her car. Maybe asking her to go over the reports tonight hadn't been such a great idea after all. Maybe she'd benefit more from making an early night of it and catching up on some rest. We'd waited this long, one more night wouldn't matter.

"You know what?" I said after a moment, pushing my empty salad bowl aside to start on my chicken. "Forget about those reports for the evening. They can wait until tomorrow. My head's too full of numbers as it is, and I could use a break, frankly."

Layla glanced up at me, a mix of relief and wariness flickering through her lovely dark gaze. "Are you sure?"

"Yes. Absolutely," I said, taking a long swig of my ale. "Let's rest tonight and start fresh in the morning."

"Okay." Her small smile was rife with gratefulness, and I felt an odd pressure in my chest. Protectiveness and appreciation. "If you're sure, then I wouldn't mind an early night either. I'll check my schedule after dinner, and we can set up a time that works for both of us."

SEVEN
DRAKE

"We want Shepperton in our portfolio of companies," Mark Walden told me the next day. He and his son, Clint, sat across the table from me in the boardroom. "I think our business philosophies mesh well together and we can take things even farther toward your family's original vision—bringing the business to new markets while making adjustments to keep costs under control would allow Shepperton, Inc. to grow stockholder value to new heights. Win-win, am I right?"

This was the first meeting with prospective buyers on my agenda, and I had to say I wasn't impressed. Mark and Clint reminded me way too much of my own father and Devon. That was bad. Sure, they talked about expanding the company's operations, but behind the fancy language, I knew that "adjustments" to costs inevitably meant finding cheaper labor markets and cutting jobs. Sure, it would grow the company's bottom line, but at the expense of all the decent workers who had made this company into the industry powerhouse it was. What I wanted to do was tell them both to take their portfolio and shove it where the sun didn't shine. What I did instead was steeple my fingers and tap the tips against my lips while taking a deep breath and praying for patience. There had to be better buyers out there. People who wouldn't chop up the assets and sell them to the highest bidder, or lay off whole communities of dedicated employees. Devon and my father might not have cared about the people working for them, but I did. In fact, the employees were about the only thing I did care about at Shepperton. Well, that and Layla.

In a purely professional and protector capacity.

Yep.

I shifted in my seat and crossed my legs away from Mark Walden and his son. "Well, you've certainly given me a lot to think about." I pressed the button on the intercom to have Maggie show them out. "I'll be in touch if I need anything else from you."

Before they could protest the abrupt ending to our meeting, my trusty assistant showed up to escort them to the exit. I reminded myself to give her a raise on her next paycheck.

"Oh." Maggie stopped with the door nearly closed behind her and peeked her head back into the boardroom. "Ms. Bailey's here to see you as well."

My dreary morning turned a bit sunnier. "Send her to my office, please."

"Will do, Drake," Maggie said smiling.

Layla

I sat in one of the overpriced designer chairs Devon had recently redecorated the reception area outside of his office with and fussed with the pristine hem of my white shirt. It was probably my imagination, but it seemed that already my clothes were fitting a bit tighter. Silly, honestly. I wasn't even showing yet. But still…ever since I'd found out I was pregnant, everything about my life had changed. Why not my clothing size too?

I snorted and looked up as two men came down the hall with Maggie, their voices carrying over the quiet classical music piped in over the built-in sound system in the ceiling.

"Nailed it," the younger guy said. With his slick appearance and shark-like smile, he reminded me of Devon in all the worst ways. "They'd be idiots not to sell to us. No one gives better balance sheet appeal than us."

The two men stepped aboard the elevator and the doors closed, cutting off the rest of their conversation. Still, I had heard enough to figure out they must be prospective buyers for the company. I'd known Drake was aggressively searching for new ownership, I just hadn't expected it to happen so fast, I supposed. My stomach cramped a bit, and I rubbed my hand over the sore spot. Another change coming, and one I felt less happy about. With Shepperton, Inc. changing hands, there was no guarantee the new owners would continue with the foundation arm of the business, or that they would want me to continue running it. If Shepperton, Inc. was folded into another company, there would be redundancies that resulted in job cuts, which meant I could find myself out on the street just when I needed steady income the most.

Of course, Drake had assured me I'd be taken care of, but the prospect was still unsettling. I liked my independence. Avoided being beholden to people like the plague. But was that just my pride speaking? As a mother, shouldn't I put the well-being of my child ahead of everything else? Or would I be sending the wrong message to my child if I let someone else take care of my problems instead of facing them myself?

Ugh, it was all so confusing, and I was already reeling from everything else going on.

"You can go back to his office now, Ms. Bailey," Maggie called to me.

"Thank you," I said, standing and grabbing my bag with the laptop inside. The older woman smiled at me as I passed by the reception desk, her narrowed gaze far too perceptive for my comfort. Feeling the weight of the secretary's stare on my back as I reached the hallway leading to Drake's office, I couldn't stop myself from asking, "What?"

"Nothing," Maggie said, sitting down behind her desk once more. "You just look different, that's all."

"Different how?"

"Hmm. Hard to say." Maggie peered at me over the rims of her glasses. "There's a glow about you."

I blanched slightly. No one knew I was pregnant except for me and Drake. Surely he wouldn't have said anything. And if it was too early for me be showing, it was way too early to glow, right?

Feeling flustered, I tucked my hair behind my left ear and turned away, mumbling, "Vitamins."

By the time I reached Drake's corner office, my anxiety was mounting. It would be hard enough for me to find a new job once I told a prospective employer I'd be off on maternity not long after I started. Technically, they couldn't not hire me because of it, but if it was down to me and another qualified candidate who *wasn't* pregnant…why *wouldn't* they pick the option that caused the least amount of trouble for them?

My stomach churned again, and I forced myself to calm. I'd been sick earlier this morning as it was. No sense upchucking again now, especially outside Drake's office. I took a deep breath and exhaled slowly, waiting to knock until the bile receded from my throat.

"Come in," Drake called from inside and I opened the door, halting at the sight of him behind Devon's old desk, the burn in my throat quickly replaced by a different kind of fire in my blood. At first I'd only seen the physical similarities between the brothers. Now the differences were more apparent to me than ever, in a good way. Drake was everything Devon wasn't. Good, strong, moral, kind. And, if I was honest with myself—gorgeous as hell. Yep. I was attracted to him. No doubt about it.

Not that I planned to act on that at all. I smiled, then looked away from him fast before he noticed me staring. I closed the door behind me and took a seat in the single chair left in front of the desk. The atmosphere in the room was much more relaxed than it had ever been when the previous occupant was around. Devon was almost manic when it came to his appearance, always dressed impeccably, always demanding perfection of everything around him, never satisfied with "good enough."

Drake, on the other hand, sat back in his temporary office chair while Devon's old, uncomfortable designer model had been shoved into the corner where it belonged. After his meeting he'd loosened his tie again, the first button of his shirt open to reveal a small glimpse of his tanned throat. I found myself blinking at that tiny area now, feeling a strange urge to lick him right there to see if he moaned.

Whoops. No. I had no business having my tongue anywhere near Drake Shepperton. Nope.

"So, did you have a chance to go over those reports this morning?" he asked me, playing with a stack of paper clips on his desk. "Find anything new?"

"I did," I said, glad for the distraction from staring at his muscled bod sprawled in that chair like he owned the place…which he did. But still. He carried the power so easily, so gracefully. There was no pretension with Drake, no need to prove himself to anyone, not like with Devon. He had always been so driven to prove he was number one, to stay on top, to keep his edge. Drake was comfortable in his own skin. That was it. He didn't force things because there wasn't a need to. It was one of the things I found most attractive about him. I cleared my throat of the sudden constriction there and continued. "Go over those reports from accounting again, I mean. And no. I didn't find anything new."

"Okay." Drake sat forward, shoving the paper clips aside so he could rest his forearms on the desk. "Well, keep searching the financial records. And I've got an outside analyst probing Devon's personal accounts for any irregularities. Also, I need you to give me a list of all the people who could sign off on outgoing grant money, please."

"No problem." I got out my laptop and typed notes into a new document. "What else?"

"Go over the top grants again and see if any oddities pop out at you. You'd know better than me what should and shouldn't be there."

"Done." I started to get up, but Drake stopped me.

"Unless you need to go back to your desk, you might as well work from here." He pointed to the table across the office. "It looks like it's getting ready to rain outside." Years ago, when Shepperton, Inc. had outgrown the office space in its original building, the simplest way to expand had been to purchase the building across the street. A sky bridge had long since been constructed to connect the two buildings on the upper floors, but a bad storm the previous month had caused some damage to the bridge, so for the time being, a short walk outside was needed to pass from one building to the other.

"Oh." I glanced out his window and saw the clouds increasing. It had only been overcast when I'd walked over here earlier. "Okay. Sure. I can work from here, I guess."

I got myself set up at the table, then dug into the projects Drake had given me. While I worked, he handled more of the daily tasks of the business that required the CEO's authorization, mainly phone calls and paperwork, from what I could tell. I did my best not to listen in, but with us sitting in the same room, it was impossible. As I pulled up reports and made lists, I noted the tone with which he talked to people. Courteous and clear, with none of the artifice and sarcasm that had been so evident in Devon's voice a lot of the time. Devon had been too busy, too important, for those he felt beneath him most of the time, and it had showed.

Honestly, that was another reason I'd been shocked as hell when Devon had come on to me, let alone actively pursued me, as if I was some kind of prize to be won. As my parents always used to say, you can take the girl out of the streets, but you can't take the street out of the girl. Since my eighteenth birthday, I'd worked hard to change myself inside and out into the woman I was today—poised and polished, without a hint of grifter. But Devon had shown such disgust for people who he considered beneath him, to the point where I'd worried he'd be able to sense my history somehow—hear it in my voice, or even smell it on my skin. I'd never felt entirely comfortable around him, waiting for the day he'd discover the truth about me and turn those vicious words of his against me. I'd been on guard with Devon, even in the bedroom.

The fact that I'd had dinner with Drake the night before in my bathrobe just proved how much more comfortable I was with him than I had ever been with his brother. Hell, I'd even told him about my piercings, which I never did with anyone. But there was just something about him, something that made me want to open up and share it all with him.

Or maybe that was my stupid hormones again. Hard to tell these days.

I finished the list of names and sent it to the printer, then got up to retrieve it for Drake.

"Here are the people authorized to disburse grant money," I said, laying the paper on his desk.

"Thanks." He scanned the names, frowning. "Are all these people employees?"

"Yes. It's a mix of Shepperton, Inc. finance department and foundation staff."

"Huh. Okay." He set the list aside and waved me around the desk to where he had the queries he'd run the night before pulled up on his computer screen. "We need to figure out who else might have been involved. I don't see any names in this query that aren't on your list, but that doesn't mean that every transaction is actually legit."

He hit a few keys and printed out the results. "Look at these and cross off all the ones you know are legitimate."

I got to work going through the pages, and when I was finished, I handed the stack back to him. "There's only a couple of them I don't recognize. Most of them are Devon's, but there are a couple others too. Looks like three separate people authorized those. Want me to start with reviewing those, since Devon's are already suspect?"

"Yeah. We eliminate everyone else, if we can."

We each went back to work at our stations, gathering data for several hours, until the clock on the wall chimed five. I stood and stretched while Drake scowled at his screen. Somewhere along the way, I noted, he'd shed his suit coat and was now in just shirtsleeves, the cuffs of which were rolled up to reveal his muscled, tanned forearms lightly dusted with dark hair. Things low in my belly tightened, despite my wishes, and I quickly tamped down my attraction. I was here to work, not drool over my hot new boss.

Drake glanced over at me, his dark eyes keen. "Find out about those three people?"

"Yep. Two of them, anyway. The third one, though, is a bit sketchy." I carried my notes over to his desk, glad to move around after sitting so long. "Carrie Bartlett's the one I haven't been able to clear. She used to work in accounting before being promoted to associate by Devon a few months ago. She reported directly to him and no one else. I don't have access to her employee file."

"Huh." Drake looked over my notes. "Do you know her?"

"Not really, beyond what I told you just now." I shrugged. "She didn't really have anything to do with the foundation arm of things."

"Right." He hit the button for speakerphone and dialed, then glanced at the clock. An answering machine picked up in HR and he waited for the beep before leaving his message. "Yes, this is Drake Shepperton. Please send the employment file for Carrie Bartlett to my office first thing in the morning. Also send me the records of any vacation requests or recent leave of absence records on her. Thank you."

After he hung up, Drake stood and grabbed his jacket and keys. "Ready to go home? I'm bushed."

I smiled, then stifled a yawn as I went back to the table to gather my things. "Same. And yes. Let's get out of here."

EIGHT

LAYLA

I sat at the kitchen table that night, watching while Drake whipped up yet another delicious dinner. I felt a bit guilty, actually, letting him do all the work, but he'd insisted I relax. Still, I couldn't help asking once more, "Are you sure there's nothing I can do?"

"Positive." He grinned at me over his shoulder. "Seriously. Like I said, I like doing this stuff."

From his easy posture and lighter mood, it was obvious that was true, and once again, I was struck by how different the two brothers were. One time, I had tried making shrimp scampi for us despite my lack of cooking experience and Devon had totally balked when I asked him to do even the simplest thing for me, like stir a sauce or add a pinch of salt to something. He'd considered things like cooking and cleaning to be beneath him. He'd said his time was too valuable to waste on menial chores when he could be using it to make more money. I'd teased him then, asking if that was why he'd taken on the CFO job himself. Devon had responded by surprising me, picking me up and carrying me to bed. Dinner had burned, obviously, but at the time neither of us had cared. Now, though, I wondered if the sex that night had been just one more distraction tactic on Devon's part to keep me from learning the truth about him and his misdeeds with the company finances.

"You look deep in thought," Drake said from where he stood at the stove, watching me. "Something wrong?"

"No," I said, doing my best to shake off my sudden sense of betrayal. I'd suspected for a while now what Devon had done—that his courtship of me had been nothing but a ploy all along. Silly to let it get to me so much now. Must be the tiredness I felt, or maybe hunger. Certainly not the man making me dinner because he said I needed to eat well, or the fact there was something about Drake that made me want to open up and confide in him about everything. I sighed and sat back, crossing my arms around my middle, wanting to shift the spotlight off myself. "Tell me about why you joined the Navy."

He blinked at me for a second, then shrugged. "Seemed like a good idea at the time." At my flat look, he snorted. "Fine, although that's not really a lie. It did seem like a good idea. I went to the school my parents wanted me to attend, but instead of getting the degree they demanded, I signed up for NROTC and took a course load that I thought suited me better. I knew the family business wasn't for me, so I took a different track."

"Why wasn't it for you?" I leaned an elbow on the table and rested my chin in one hand. "The way Devon talked about it, all the Sheppertons were born to it, like some divine right or something."

"See?" Drake shook his head and faced the stove once more. The delicious smell of caramelized onions and peppers and the sound of sizzling steak for our fajitas filled the room. He frowned and turned the burner down, stirring in a handful of spices. "That's exactly the kind of BS that had me running in the opposite direction from my family. Born to run a manufacturing business, like it's some kind of divine destiny? What a load of crap. I'll tell you something. The only thing I saw my brother and parents born to was a life of greed and heartlessness when it came to money." He huffed out a breath, then reached up into the cabinet to grab a platter for the fajitas. "I learned early on I wanted no part of that after what happened to my friend Billy's dad."

I ignored the rumbling in my stomach and concentrated on his story. "Who's Billy?"

"He was my best friend through high school." Drake dumped the contents of the frying pan onto the platter and placed the dirty pan in the sink. "His dad worked for Shepperton, Inc., in one of our manufacturing plants. Anyway, he was just a normal guy. Not rich or entitled or anything."

"So, not like Devon then?" I raised a brow at him, my tone snarky.

"Exactly." Drake set the steaming platter of veggies and meat on the table, then went back to the counter for the warm tortillas and toppings. I couldn't help sneaking a bite of onion once his back was turned. The flavor filled my mouth, sweet and spicy and completely delicious. I wiped my hand on the robe as he returned to the table again with plates and silverware for us. "Anyway, Billy's dad got injured at work one day. It was bad. His arm got caught in a piece of machinery, and they nearly had to amputate it."

"Oh God," I said, holding my stomach. "That's terrible."

"You want me to stop?" he asked, his gaze flicking to my abdomen. "Didn't mean to upset you."

"No. It's fine." Drake so rarely talked about himself or his past that even if his story had bothered me, which it hadn't, I would have lied, just to keep him talking. "Please go on."

He hurried over with plates and drinks, then took the chair across from me as we each filled our plates with food. "Well, my family, in their greed, tried to cut off his workers compensation benefits. They thought the costs of his hospital care and rehab were too much. They tried to say that Billy's dad was responsible for his injuries because he was negligent."

"How awful. They said he caused his own accident?"

"Pretty much. Billy's dad sued, as he should have, and went to court, but he couldn't afford the best lawyers like my family could. The Shepperton attorneys dug up a bunch of stuff about Billy's mom. She'd been sick for a while with MS and Billy's dad was her primary caretaker. They used that in court against him. Said his exhaustion made him less careful. Said he didn't go through the proper checklists before operating his machinery. Said if he'd been well-rested and acting responsibly, he wouldn't have gotten hurt. Lying bastards."

I nibbled on a tortilla and frowned. "Was he at fault?"

"No. Not at all." Drake tore into his fajita-stuffed burrito with more viciousness than necessary. He chewed and swallowed before answering, visibly forcing himself to speak calmly. "Billy's dad did absolutely nothing wrong. In fact, I went to the factory myself to look at the maintenance records on that machine, once I found out what was going on. That was when I learned that Shepperton didn't keep that equipment in good repair at all. The fittings were outdated, and it was only a matter of time until they failed. Billy's dad just had the misfortune to be in the wrong place at the wrong time. I went to my family with that information, stupidly thinking that it might sway them to make a fairer decision, but it didn't. They just gave my facts to their attorneys who then buried them so deep no one would ever find them again. Billy's family went bankrupt trying to fight for compensation and my family and Shepperton, Inc. walked away owing nothing. That was the final straw. I knew I could never work for the company after that. Even now, remembering it turns my stomach."

"Wow. That's…" I swallowed hard. "I don't even have words for how bad that is."

"Right?" He finished his fajita and started making another, his dark brows furrowed. "Bet if you'd known that going in, you'd never have gotten involved with Shepperton, Inc.—or with my brother, huh?"

I took a deep breath, the question of why exactly I'd slept with Devon Shepperton swirling in my head, as it had been since I'd first discovered his deceit.

"Sorry," Drake said a moment later. "Forget I said that last part. Your choices about my brother are your own business." He filled his tortilla with veggies and meat, then put the fork back on the platter. "It just pisses me off so much, the things my family got away with because of our money."

"Understandable." I finished my plate and pushed it away, my appetite appeased for now. I frowned, toying with my glass of sparkling water. "And I can see now why you'd rather join the Navy than be a part of that legacy."

"Yep." He finished another bite of food and took a swig of his ale. "Honestly, being a SEAL has been the best part of my life. Traveling the world, experiencing other cultures, giving back through my service. I've loved every minute of it. Even when awful things happen, I know I can count on my team. I would rather stick it out with them, even through hard times, than be involved in Shepperton Inc. I feel like I've really *made* something of my life, you know? Righting wrongs and restoring justice in the world."

"That's…really inspiring, Drake. Really." And it only made my own past stand out in sharper contrast. In truth, I suspected I knew exactly why I'd gotten involved with Devon Shepperton. It wasn't because of his money or his flashy clothes or cars or even the fact he was drop-dead handsome. Nope. The secret behind Devon's appeal to me had been what he'd represented. Stability. After years of living on the run with my parents, never knowing where the next meal was coming from or when the cops might show up on our doorstep, being with a man who seemed to have it all together had been far too tempting to resist. I pushed back my chair and stood, carrying my dishes to the sink and sneaking a glance at Drake from beneath my lashes. Too bad I'd chosen the wrong brother. Devon might appear to be a catch on paper, but Drake was the real deal. A good man through and through. "How long do you plan to stay in the Navy now?"

"As long as they'll have me," he said, wiping his mouth with a napkin. "As long as I can serve."

I nodded and turned away, reality slapping me upside the head. The fact was I had no business swooning over Drake Shepperton, no matter how wonderful he might be. He'd be leaving again as soon as he found a buyer for the company, and I'd be on my own again to deal with the pregnancy and my future as a single mom. Best not to start down that road with him to begin with. I'd been heartbroken enough for one lifetime, thanks so much. I forced a smile I didn't quite feel as I rinsed my plate to put it in the dishwasher.

Drake

"I can get the rest of this," I said, moving in beside Layla at the sink a short time later. My skin tingled as she brushed against me, and I tamped down my reaction hard. Living with her like this, sharing our space and opening up about our pasts, was more intimate than I'd expected. Worse, I liked it. And that was dangerous stuff, considering our current predicament and the fact she was carrying my brother's baby. So, instead of letting my forbidden desires grow, I changed subjects while she took a seat back at the table. I wanted to know more about her but didn't want to pry, so I talked about what I hoped was a safer topic. The foundation. "What's your game plan for organizations to sponsor in the next quarter? Got your eye on anything new?"

"No. Not yet." She sighed and I felt that breathy sound clear to my toes. "Honestly, I'm afraid things will be more difficult than ever with Devon gone."

"Why's that?" I asked as I washed the pans and utensils I'd cooked with.

"Because if this gets out, no one's going to want to deal with a charity that's tainted by scandal." She hung her head, her dark brows knitted. "Besides, who knows if there will even be a foundation once the new owners take possession of the company? There's a chance I won't even have a job when the sale's all done and dusted."

My mind went back to the two idiots I'd talked to earlier that morning and knew they'd never think about giving away their cash to those less fortunate. One more reason to cross them off the list of potential buyers, as far as I was concerned. Good riddance. But there was still the truth that no matter who I ended up selling Shepperton, Inc. to, they might not want the burden of a charity and all the paperwork and regulations that went with a non-profit along with the company. And once I signed on the dotted line, I'd have no say in the new owner's decision at all. I could, however, ease at least one of Layla's fears for now. "Well, regardless of what happens, my offer holds. I'll make sure you and the baby are taken care of. It's the least I can do."

She shook her head, not meeting my gaze. "Thank you, but the baby and I will be fine. My biggest concern right now is getting to the bottom of this financial mess, so I don't have to keep looking over my shoulder. I don't like being afraid."

The fear in her voice made my chest squeeze tighter, as did the paleness of her face. She stood to walk into the living room and without thinking, I took her hand, stopping her. I stepped closer, near enough to feel her warmth and smell the floral scent of her shampoo. Her brown eyes had tiny flecks of gold in them. How had I not noticed that before? Her soft pink lips parted, and tiny lines of confusion formed between her raised brows. Before I could stop myself, I rushed on. "You don't have to be afraid, Layla. I'm here and I'll protect you, no matter what. No one will harm you or the baby under my watch, I promise."

Her cheeks colored and I started to reach up to brush my fingertips over her velvety skin before I stopped myself. "Thank you," she said. "I appreciate all you're doing for me."

Layla swayed slightly toward me, and I put my other hand on her waist to steady her. This close, her warm breath fanned across my face and her breasts brushed against my chest. My throat dried and my words creaked out past the lump of need constricting my vocal cords. "If you want, I can move you into one of the open offices down the hall from mine tomorrow. That way we can go over the information we need to without the hassle of going to one location or the other. We'll be together."

Her eyes dropped to my lips, her pupils blown wide, as she murmured back my last word. "Together."

Maybe it was the stress. Maybe it was the crazy situation we were in. Maybe it was just the moment, but whatever it was, I leaned in and kissed her, needing to taste Layla more than I needed my next breath. She let me in, her mouth opening beneath the pressure of my lips and her tongue sliding against mine. I groaned low and pulled her tighter against me. It was too much. It would never be enough. It was…

Over.

Layla placed her hands on my shoulders and pushed hard, breaking us apart. Her face was flushed, and her lips were swollen from my kiss. She looked wild and wanton and as confused by what had just happened as I felt. I dropped my hands to the sides and fisted them to keep from reaching for her again, my pulse racing a mile a minute.

"I, uh…" Layla tucked her hair behind her ear, those piercings of hers twinkling at him like a cosmic joke. "I'm going to hit the sack. Goodnight."

I watched her go, knowing it was just an excuse to bail. Hell, it wasn't even eight o'clock yet. Still, considering how my body had tightened and how my heart ached to be with her, she'd made the right choice. I needed to keep my hands to myself and my heart out of the picture where Layla was concerned if I wanted to get all of us out of this mess unscathed.

NINE
DRAKE

I got ready the next morning and wondered exactly when I'd lost my damned mind. Each time I closed my eyes, all I could think of was the kiss with Layla. How she'd tasted, the velvet of her skin, those tiny mewls she'd made before she sank into me. It was enough to drive a sane man crazy. It sure as hell had kept me up all night, tossing and turning.

God. What a fucking mess.

I rubbed my eyes and sat back on the edge of the bed to stare up at the ceiling. The fact was I was wildly attracted to Layla Bailey even if I shouldn't be. She had been with my brother, for fuck's sake. She was carrying Devon's baby. And sure, she'd confirmed point-blank to me that her time with my brother had been nothing but sex, no emotional entanglement at all, but that shouldn't matter.

Should it?

Restless, I sat forward again and did my best to shove all that drama aside and focus on the financial reports I'd requested. Devon had really gone all out trying to hide what he was doing, that was for sure. Taking over as CFO, burying his phony charity transactions under a mountain of extraneous paperwork. Would've worked too, if it hadn't been for Layla.

That idea snagged in my head. Devon was crafty as hell. Was it possible his affair with Layla had been just another ploy to throw her off his scent? I couldn't imagine anyone not wanting Layla, but considering the number of women my brother had been with during his lifetime and the ruthless way my family tended to use people, the notion wasn't completely out of left field.

The thought of poor Layla getting caught up in the web of Devon's filthy schemes made my stomach turn. She was a good person. Honest and forthright and true. She deserved better than that. Especially given her current situation. I couldn't imagine the pressure she must be under, facing single motherhood. And yes, I'd offered her financial help—which she kept declining—but I knew little about what other support she might have once the baby arrived. She'd told me little about herself or her past. Not that I wanted to pry or anything, but I was curious.

More curious than you should be...

Sounds echoed down the hall from the kitchen, jarring me from my thoughts. A glance at the clock showed it was nearly seven-thirty. We'd be late if we didn't get a move on. I slid on my loafers and fixed my tie, then grabbed my suit jacket before heading down the hall to find Layla standing in front of the toaster, a travel mug of tea in her hand.

"Morning," she said, not meeting my gaze. "You hungry?"

I was, but not for food. To distract myself, I headed into the living room instead and clicked on the TV to watch the latest financial news update. I really couldn't care less how the markets were doing in Hong Kong, but it was better than embarrassing myself because I couldn't stop imagining picking Layla up and setting her on the counter, kissing her silly as she wrapped those long, shapely legs of hers around my waist...

"No," I said, the words emerging harsher than I'd intended. I cleared my throat and tried again. "I'm fine, thanks. You about ready to go?"

"Yeah." Her toast popped up in the toaster and she turned to butter it. "Just let me grab a napkin so I can munch on this on the way. Unless you don't want food in your car."

"It's fine." I turned back to the TV, away from the view that showed me how that blue pantsuit of hers hugged her hips to perfection and cupped her butt just so. Man, I had it bad for this woman and that wasn't good. "Bring whatever you want."

"Great." She joined me in the living room a minute or so later, her bag over her shoulder and her mug in one hand, toast wrapped in a napkin in the other. "Ready."

"Awesome."

The ride in to the office felt anything but awesome, though. We both avoided discussing the kiss as if it was a live grenade ready to explode, and instead chatted about the weather or the road construction happening everywhere or other stupid subjects. I didn't pay much attention, my senses far too attuned to Layla to really allow me to concentrate on small talk. Lord help me, even the way she ate turned me on, licking those crumbs off her lips with that pink tongue of hers. I envisioned all the ways I'd like her to use that tongue on me, which only made my blood pound harder than it already was. At this rate, I'd have a coronary by noon.

Once I parked in my designated spot and helped Layla from the car, it was after eight. Maggie was smiling behind her desk, as usual, when we walked in.

"Good morning, Drake, Ms. Bailey," Maggie said. "I've got your messages here for you, Drake."

"Thanks." I stopped at the desk and grabbed the stack of post-its she handed me. "Can you please have the empty office next to mine prepared for Ms. Bailey's use for the duration of my stay here?"

"Uh," the assistant said, the surprise on her face quickly masked behind her usual expression of efficient politeness. "Of course. I'll call maintenance right now."

"Thank you, Maggie," I said, already heading down the hall toward my office with Layla by my side. "Let me know when it's ready. Until then, Layla will share my space with me."

"Of course," Maggie called from behind us. "They say it will be about an hour."

"Perfect." I opened the door and stood aside for Layla to enter first. As she passed, her sweet floral scent tickled my nose before I tamped down my awareness. This was a place of business, and we had a full day of work ahead of us. This wasn't the time or the place to get distracted by how amazing she smelled. I got Layla set up at the table where she'd worked earlier, then went back to the reception area. "Oh, and Maggie, can you get me access to Devon's storage unit at the penthouse? All the residents have one, but I haven't been able to locate my brother's key."

"Sure thing," Maggie said. "I'll call the building security for you."

"Thanks."

The rest of the day passed quickly, between phone calls and meetings and getting Layla set up in her office beside mine. She'd still have to go back to her usual office space for staff meetings and the like, but so much of her work with her team was done via phone calls and emails that it didn't really matter where she worked. I worked through lunch to get through my stack of messages and ended up finishing my work around the same time Layla did, so she didn't have to wait on me, since we'd ridden together.

I was just finishing up with my final phone call of the day when Layla knocked on my door, her bag in hand. I waved her inside and pointed to the chairs in front of my desk, indicating she should sit and wait for me.

"Any chance I could get those records faster?" I asked the man on the phone. I was speaking to the outside CPA firm that acted as independent oversight for the Shepperton family when it came to taxes and such. I'd asked them to look into Devon's personal holdings for me. If my brother was in as deep with the money laundering scam as I suspected, then it made sense to check every corner. "I'll pay whatever added cost is necessary, but I really need that information ASAP."

Layla leaned forward and I placed my hand over the receiver to hear her say, "I need to use the restroom before we go. I'll meet you in the lobby."

I nodded and watched her leave while the accountant on the phone quoted him a ridiculous amount to get the reports I wanted by the next day. Under normal circumstances, I would have balked at the cost, just as a matter of principle, but this was hardly business as usual. And it wasn't like I couldn't afford it. "Fine. I'll have the cash wired over tomorrow. Thank you."

I met Layla in the lobby and after saying goodnight to Maggie, we headed back to the condo. Both of us were quiet. I worried that things would always be awkward as hell now because of that kiss. I was still berating himself internally for screwing up so badly when she tilted her head to look out the window beside her.

"New moon will be here soon," she said, peering out into the gathering twilight.

Slowing for a red light, I glanced over at her. "You follow the moon phases?"

"Sure. I love astronomy." She settled back into her seat. "Why?"

"No reason." The light turned green, and I accelerated through the intersection. "I like space too."

"Yeah?" She grinned. "When I was a kid, I used to spend a lot of time alone, watching the night sky. Tracking the stars. As I got older, I wanted to learn more about all of it."

"Me too!" I smiled and flipped my signal, turning onto the street where the condo was located. "When I was growing up, I hated all the fancy parties my parents used to throw at our house. Devon, of course, loved them."

"Of course." Layla rolled her eyes and we both laughed.

"Anyway, while they had their galas downstairs, I used to go up on the roof by myself and use my telescope. I got some books from the library and taught myself about the constellations and other galaxies and stuff. I still love to stargaze, when I have the time."

"Same." She rubbed her hand over her abdomen absently as she spoke.

"Everything okay?" I asked, concerned.

"Fine." She gave me a sad little smile. "Just imagining sharing that love with my baby someday."

"That would be cool." Relief eased the tension in my shoulders, and I rested one elbow near the window beside me. "I haven't had a chance to check out the skies around Dallas lately, but with the city lights, it's not optimal viewing. You'd have to get outside the city limits to have a proper look."

"Agreed. There's a state park not far away that usually has a good turnout from the local astronomy club for the new moon. You can see Andromeda and the Pleiades too, on a good night."

"Wow. That sounds great."

"It is." She rested her head back against the seat as dusk fell. "I've been a few times and it's pretty cool. They have weekend retreats where the park rangers act as guides and help people pick out the different galaxies and star clusters."

"I'd love that." I turned into the garage for the condo and parked, then cut the engine. It felt like forever since I'd just relaxed and studied the stars. It used to be one of my favorite things to do on missions, when I wasn't working or learning about the local cuisine. The fact that Layla also loved astronomy made me happier than anything had in a long time. A crazy idea entered my head and before I could stop myself it spilled out of my mouth. "You said they have the weekend retreats to coincide with the new moon?"

She nodded, giving me some side-eye. "Yep. Why?"

I rushed ahead before I couldn't. "Want to go with me?"

Her dark brows rose and she met my gaze directly. "On a camping retreat? To the state park? This weekend? Together?"

I swallowed hard. "Yes. I mean, only if you want to. I just thought it might be nice to get away from all this Devon business and just relax for a change. It could be fun, just you and me. Not like a date," I quickly amended when her lovely eyes widened. "I mean… Yes, we'd go together, but as friends. Camping buddies. Fellow stargazers. That's all."

Layla blinked at me a long moment, and my chest squeezed with an odd mix of wariness and anticipation. Honestly, I hadn't felt this nervous since I'd been in high school asking the prettiest girl in school to go to prom with me. I'd lived and died in those few seconds waiting for her answer back then (which had been yes) and now wasn't any different. Heat crept up from beneath the collar of my white dress shirt and I desperately wanted to loosen my tie, but didn't want to fidget and give away my anxiety.

Finally, she gave a small nod and a smile. "I'd like that. To go to the state park with you, I mean. It'll be nice to get out of the condo for a while."

"Great." I got out of the car and walked around to open the door for her. Warmth buzzed in my stomach before I tamped it down. "It's a date then. No. I mean not a date," I fumbled. "I mean…"

"I know what you meant," Layla said, winking at me over her shoulder as she walked to the entrance to the condo. "I'm looking forward to it."

"Me too." I unlocked the door to let her in, then hesitated on the threshold, feeling like we'd just taken a step forward. Toward what, I wasn't sure, but damn if I wasn't excited to find out.

TEN

LAYLA

By the time Saturday rolled around, I had changed my mind at least a million times about going camping with Drake. Sometimes I wanted to go, badly. I enjoyed thinking about the good conversations we'd had, how easy it felt to be around him, his kindness and consideration and protectiveness toward me. All those were good things that made me want to spend more time with him. But then I'd remember that kiss we'd shared in the kitchen, the way my knees had gone weak the moment he'd touched me, how heat and need had surged through my bloodstream. Whenever that happened, my fears took hold as I worried over him being Devon's brother and a Shepperton and therefore not exactly the best bet as far as a long-term prospect was concerned. With that in mind, I wondered if I should be keeping my distance. It had been enough to drive me to drink. Or, since there was the baby to think of, eat massive amounts of chocolate cookies instead.

Ugh.

Now though, as I walked beside him up the short distance to the clearing at the top of the hill where the view of the sky was best, I felt confident I'd made the right choice in coming. I could handle whatever this weekend threw my way. We'd parked his rental SUV in the parking lot near the start of the path, Drake insisting he wanted me on my feet as little as possible.

"Are you sure I can't help carry anything?" I asked, glancing over at him weighed down with gear. To his credit, he seemed to have no problems with the load of stuff in his arms or strapped over his brawny shoulders. "I'm pregnant, not an invalid."

"I've got it," he said, adjusting his backpack with one hand while toting the case with the telescope in it in the other. That pack alone had to weigh at least fifty pounds, but he made it look light as a feather. My traitorous heart fluttered at the thought of all that muscle lurking beneath his plaid flannel work shirt and tight jeans. "Besides, you *are* carrying something."

"A map doesn't count."

"Sure it does. Without it, we'd have no clue where to get the best seats."

We crested the top of the hill and found lots of other people already setting up their equipment for the evening. I checked my watch. Almost seven-thirty. Dusk had started to fall, and the sun would disappear soon. Best find a spot and get to it. After consulting the map together, we chose a patch of open ground near the west side of the clearing, twenty feet or so from the closest observer. Enough space to have a bit of privacy, but not so far away that we were too isolated.

Drake set the backpack on the ground and started setting up the telescope while I unpacked the things we'd brought along—a white light to help us when we weren't stargazing; a red light to help our eyes adjust when we were looking skyward; insect repellent; bottled waters and snacks. I set it all out atop the sturdy wool blanket I'd packed, then set up our two folding chairs.

"How's the telescope coming?" I asked, opening a plastic baggie full of carrots and pulling one out to munch on. "Anything I can help with?"

"Nope. I think I'm done," he said, leaning over to peer through the oculus to make a few adjustments to the lens. The light was dimming—but it wasn't dim enough to hide his form, and damn if I could stop myself from checking out his taut butt and long legs. He really was a certified stud. Handsome, smart, and sexy as hell, especially when he got absorbed in something that interested him. Honestly, one of the main reasons I'd jumped on his offer of moving me into an office next door to his was because sitting in the same room with him while he worked had gotten far too distracting. There was a certain expression that came over his gorgeous features when he concentrated, quiet intelligence mixed with masterful wits, that made the need to be near him almost overwhelming. I'd always been drawn to men who were confident and competent at what they did. It was probably one of the main things that had drawn me initially to Devon. He might have been a lying turd behind the scenes, but in his office, in his position as figurehead for Shepperton Inc., he'd exuded a high-wattage self-confidence that had been hard to resist, even for a skeptic like me.

Drake, though, had a quieter power that was less in your face. Sure, he was hot and charming, but there was a reserve about him. You didn't get past the charismatic shell until you knew him better and then, look out! I sighed and narrowed my gaze on him, remembering the way his hands had felt on me as he'd held me close in the kitchen, the brush of his lips against mine, the taste of ale and desire on his lips.

"You still awake over there?" he asked, looking back at me over his shoulder, one brow raised as if he'd caught me red-handed with my naughty thoughts. "Doing okay?"

Not trusting my voice, I nodded and shoved another baby carrot in my mouth. Heat prickled my cheeks, and I prayed the growing darkness was enough to cover what had to be a hellacious blush on my cheeks.

Thankfully, if Drake had noticed anything, he didn't mention it—just took the seat beside me and crunched on a carrot or two of his own.

"Won't be long now until the stars are out," he said, staring up at the darkening sky.

Soon enough, pinpricks of light began to twinkle above us, and a hush fell over the gathered crowd as people began looking up. Drake and I took turns at the telescope, marveling over the Big Dipper and Orion's Belt and the bright smudge of the Andromeda Galaxy millions of light years away.

"You ever visited a Dark Sky site like this one?" Drake asked me once I straightened from my turn at the telescope.

"I have, actually," I answered without thinking, then could have kicked myself. I hadn't meant to divulge more about my past, but now that it was out there, I couldn't take it back.

"Really?" His dark eyes glittered with curiosity in the dim red light. "This one or one nearby? I thought they were pretty rare in this day and age."

I sighed and did my best to ease the knot of tension in my chest. Drake was safe, I could confide in him, a little bit at least. "No, not here. In California. There was a Dark Sky Sanctuary near where my grand-mother lived, so when I'd go to visit her, we'd take a trip there. I used to love those times with her."

Grief pinched my chest at the memory of the Nanna I'd lost after my parents had gone to prison. My grandmother wasn't dead, just wanted nothing to do with me anymore. Not after what I'd done.

Drake must have misinterpreted the sadness on my face because he said, "I'm sorry. When did she pass?"

I started to say that the woman wasn't dead—well, not literally—but stopped myself. Mentioning some obscure fact about my youth was one thing. Opening up to him about the cesspool of my family life was another. Rather than telling a complete lie, I went with a half-truth. "It's been twelve years since I saw her last."

"That's tough." He sat back in his chair, the metal creaking beneath his bulk. "It's nice that you have astronomy to remember her by, though."

"Yeah." Happy to have the spotlight off of me once more, I tucked my hair behind one ear and crossed my sneaker-clad feet at the ankles, stretching my legs out in front of me. "Studying the stars made me feel a lot less lonely as a kid." I gave him a side glance, noting his pensive expression in the shadows from our red light as he stared up at the sky. "What about you? Have you been to a Dark Sky Reserve before?"

"Yep. Both here in the US and overseas." He took a deep breath and exhaled slowly, closing his eyes. "They're harder and harder to come by these days, with all the industrialization in the world. Places with low levels of natural light are disappearing fast. Makes the ones we have left that much more precious, I suppose."

"True." My heart pinched at the loneliness in his voice. It was a feeling I knew well, and I wanted nothing more than to bring back his smile if only for a little while. It was such a great smile, after all. I stood and went to the telescope again to gaze up at the stars. "This is really great. Thanks again for bringing me here this weekend. Lately, the best I've been able to do is visiting the local planetarium in Dallas once a month to get my space fix."

He snorted and cracked open one eye. "Space fix? I like that. It is kind of addicting, isn't it?"

"Worse than crack for me." I grinned and he did too, his teeth white and even in the darkness, and my world brightened a bit.

The next few hours passed with more viewing of the stars and small talk. We even had an impromptu picnic on the blanket with Drake making s'mores using the heat from our red light and a lighter to melt the marshmallows and chocolate bars. A trick he'd learned in the SEALs, he said.

Finally, I yawned, and Drake began breaking down the telescope while I packed up the backpack. It had been a great night and I felt more relaxed than I had in months. All thanks to Drake. By the time we'd walked down the hill to the SUV again, I felt closer to him than I had to anyone in a long, long time.

"Right." He closed the back of the SUV and faced me in the darkness. "Guess it's time we head back to the campsite."

"Guess it is," I said, my feet refusing to move from where I stood a few inches from him. My gaze flickered to his lips, then back to his eyes. All the reasons why getting involved with Drake was a bad idea were swirling in my head, but all my heart wanted to do at that moment was lose myself in him, even if only for one night. Honestly, what was the worst that could happen? I was already pregnant, so that was off the table. And he'd be leaving as soon as the mess with Shepperton, Inc. was cleared up and the business was sold, so there would be no strings attached. My blood pounded in my ears and heat sizzled through my core. Maybe it was the hormones. Maybe it was the fact that for the first time in forever I'd opened up to someone in some way, however small, and it hadn't been horrible. Maybe it was the night or the new moon magic that seemed to be stirring around us. Whatever it was, I threw caution to the winds and leaned in to kiss him again before I could stop myself.

Drake didn't move a muscle at first, seeming to be fighting an inner battle similar to the one I'd waged and lost, before he gave a low groan and wrapped his arms around me, pressing me tight to his chest and deepening our kiss.

His hands seemed to be everywhere at once—in my hair, down my back, cupping my butt through my jeans. By the time he pulled back, we were both breathless and shaking. He rested his forehead against mine and closed his eyes, his words strained. "We shouldn't…"

"True," I said, sliding my hands around his neck to trace tiny circles through the hair at his nape. Drake's answering shiver made me smile. So strong and yet so sensitive. I kissed him again lightly then smiled. "But I think we are."

He opened his eyes and stared at me a moment before cursing under his breath. "Get in the car."

I giggled and did as he asked, barely getting my seatbelt fastened before he took off in a spray of gravel for the campsite. He kept one hand on my knee as he drove, as if unable to resist touching me for one second. I felt the same, stroking his forearm and tracing his long, tapered fingers with mine.

By the time we got back to our tent, neither of us could move fast enough. Forget the telescope and the backpack in the SUV—we barely made it safely inside the tent and zipped the flap shut behind us before we were all over each other. Between kisses and sighs, Drake removed my clothes first, and then his, stopping to worship every inch of me before laying me down gently atop the air mattress and joining me, stretching out his big, beautiful body beside me. Even then, he didn't rush, kissing me long and slow before bending to take one of my nipples into his mouth while lavishing attention on the other with his talented fingers.

I slid my hands into his hair, biting back my cries of pleasure, not wanting to alert the campers around us to what we were doing. The silence only seemed to make the experience more intense. Each lick, each stroke, each caress shimmered through me like pure light, sending showers of firework sparks blazing through my nerve endings.

Drake kissed his way down my body to my abdomen, then lower still, until he traced his tongue up the slick fold between my legs, and I thought I'd died and gone to heaven. While I wasn't a virgin by any means, being with Drake felt different from any lover I'd had before. His consideration and kindness extended to the bedroom as well, with him making sure I was comfortable and happy and satisfied before he took his own pleasure. He nuzzled and made love to me with his hands and mouth until I tumbled over the brink into orgasm, unable to keep from whispering his name over and over as the waves of ecstasy rocked my entire being.

At last, he kissed his way up my body again, stopping to nuzzle my breasts once more before propping himself up on one elbow while reaching into his duffle bag for a condom. I watched him slick it on, stopping him to use my own hand to stroke his hard length. He pulled my hand away after a moment, lines of tension etched into the corners of the mouth and eyes. Drake kissed my palm, then looked down at me, his expression serious. "Are you sure about this, Layla?"

In answer, I drew him down for an open-mouthed kiss while wrapping my legs around his waist and arching my hips into him. He entered me in one long stroke, then held still, allowing my body to adjust to his. When he did move at last, we both moaned deeply and began a rhythm that had us teetering on the brink in no time at all.

"Drake, I…" I began before I climaxed once more, words lost as my universe exploded into a million iridescent shards. He drove into me once, twice more, then his body tightened in my arms as he came hard inside me, his face buried in my neck and my name on his lips.

Afterward, we lay in the darkness, listening to the crickets outside, his head resting in the valley between my breasts, over my heart, and my fingers in his hair, tracing lazy circles against his scalp. I felt sated and relaxed for the first time in recent memory and I had Drake to thank for that. I opened my mouth to tell him so, but he started speaking first, his frown returning, deepening.

"I know I gave you my usual spiel before about why I joined the SEALs," he said, his voice quiet in the shadows. "Honor, glory, all that. And it's true. But there were other reasons too. Ones I don't talk about much. Want to hear them?"

I couldn't really see his face in the dark, but the vulnerability in his tone made my heart clench. Whatever it was, he needed to tell me and I needed to hear it. I reached out to place my hand on his warm, solid chest, felt the steady thump of his pulse. "Only if you want tell me."

He gave a sad little sigh and gathered me closer. "I do. Want to tell you." We lay there for a minute before he continued. "The biggest reason was so I could build my own life. One I could be proud of. One outside of my family and all their drama."

I nodded, contemplating telling him more about my own past. It wasn't something I shared with anyone, really. Not exactly dinner conversation to tell someone you put your own parents behind bars, was it? But being with Drake, like this, it felt safe. "I get that. I built my own life too, away from my past."

"Hmm." The sound rumbled beneath my ear, warm and deep. "Yeah, I had way more than enough lies and scandal and drama growing up. I want nothing but truth and honesty and trust in my future. No more drama or greed or deception. I'm done with all of that."

"…Right." The heat in my blood from the afterglow of our lovemaking turned to ice, making me shudder. Drake pulled me closer and nestled my head under his chin, pulling the covers over us. The bright security I'd felt with him moments earlier fizzled out to blackness. I came from nothing but scandal. My whole existence had come from lies, thanks to my parents and their stealing and cheating. Drake was right. He had been through enough of that. There was no place for me in his future, not with my history. If I told him the truth about my childhood, about my parents and the part I'd played in their cons—he'd walk away right now and never want to see me again. In a way, I felt like I was deceiving him just by staying quiet. But…was I really doing any harm? There was no potential for anything lasting here—this could never be more than a fling. And that meant he didn't truly need to know my secrets. With a sigh, I snuggled closer into his heat, knowing soon enough it would be gone.

"Goodnight," Drake said, kissing the top of my head before drifting off to sleep.

I lay awake long afterward, trying not to feel heartbroken and even more alone than before. I'd known this wouldn't work out long-term. I had no right to cry about it now. No matter how badly it hurt.

ELEVEN
DRAKE

On Monday evening, I stood before the door to my brother's storage unit. It was located in the basement of Devon's condo building. Layla stood by my side, as she had since our weekend together. I still had a hard time believing it was all real. I'd never intended to sleep with her, but now that it had happened, I couldn't say I regretted it. Holding her in my arms, feeling her soft warmth beneath me, around me, had been so much better than I'd ever imagined, and I knew that no matter how this all ended between us, I'd carry those memories with me forever.

Even now, when I licked my lips, I swore I could still taste her there, could still smell the heady scent of her arousal mixed with her sweet floral perfume, could still hear her soft moans of desire echoing in my ears whenever she was near. My chest squeezed with more than attraction, more than affection. I wasn't ready yet to put a name to the emotions blustering through me like a storm front, but they were there all the same, growing stronger each day.

"What is this place?" Layla asked, her hand brushing against me and sending sparks of awareness through my already keyed-up nervous system.

"Devon's private storage area," I said, my voice gruff from a mix of adrenaline and anxiety. "It's the last place of his I haven't searched yet."

I could feel the weight of her stare on me, tingling against the side of my face. "Do you think we'll find anything in there about the financials?"

"No idea. But there's still a lot of information we don't have." I fiddled with the key in my hand that the superintendent had given me earlier. We'd just gotten home from the office when the guy had knocked on the door. Layla and I had changed and come down here right away before eating dinner. "Maybe the answers we need are in here."

As if sensing my inner turmoil, Layla took my hand and laced her fingers through mine "Let's open it and find out."

With a determined nod, I stepped forward, inserted the key into the lock, and turned it. A sharp click sounded in the quiet hallway, bouncing off the bare cement floors and walls. I let go of Layla to stoop and hoist up the metal garage door sealing off the secure space, then stood back to gaze inside, my eyes widening slightly. I'd been expecting boxes of documents and files. Instead, this place looked like a mini war room, complete with a desk and computer. Devon must have come down here and worked at night. The room was maybe ten by twelve and the walls were lined with file cabinets. If my brother was hiding the truth anywhere, this looked like the place to find it. My mood grim, I strode straight for the desk. "Did my brother ever mention this place to you?"

"Nope." She shook her head, her sleek bobbed hair flying around her face. "Believe me, if I'd known this was down here, I'd have told you to track down the key as soon as possible."

"I believe you," I said, taking a seat behind the desk to rifle through the contents of the drawers while I waited for the computer to boot up. In one of them I found a burner phone. I pulled it out and punched the home button to find a long list of alerts lighting up the screen, all of them dated the week of Devon's accident. "Damn. Looks like someone was trying pretty hard to get ahold of my brother."

"Who?" Layla came around the desk to peer over my shoulder. "Carrie Bartlett."

"Yep." I laid the phone on the desk, then hit play for the voicemail messages and put them on speakerphone. The first four were all business-related, regarding various deals in the works at Shepperton, Inc. The final one confirmed a suspicion that I had kept to myself before now, though it had been gaining more credence by the day. Carrie was having an affair with my brother.

"Hey," Carrie's overly chipper voice said from the device. "Me again. Just wanted to say I can't wait for our trip to LA together. It's going to be even better than last time, since we don't have to hide anymore."

I frowned down at the phone, then shut it off. "Sounds like something more than work was going on between those two."

"Agreed." Layla turned away fast, but not before I saw the hurt in her expression.

For a moment, my heart nosedived to my toes. She'd said there was no emotional connection between her and Devon and she'd known about his lies, but given her reaction to that message, she'd not known about his sleeping around. I had no right to be jealous, especially of a dead man, and yet I didn't like knowing my brother hurt Layla. Not at all. Best get it out then, instead of letting resentment fester. "What?"

She shook her head, causing the light to glitter in those earrings of hers studding her lobes. A sudden flash of memory of me nuzzling said ears flickered in my mind before I shoved it away. "Nothing. It's just that the first time Devon went to LA with Carrie, we were still sleeping together."

"Oh." I blinked at her a minute as understanding dawned. Even if Layla hadn't been in love with my brother, that was still a hell of a slap in the face to learn that a lover had been unfaithful. God, Devon had been even more of a treacherous asshole than I had suspected. I swallowed hard around the lump of disgust in my throat. "I'm sorry."

Layla gave a small shrug and a sad little smile. "It's not your fault. Honestly, I shouldn't be surprised. Given who and what Devon was, I had no reason to think he'd be exclusive to me during our affair. I'm madder at myself, I suppose, for not figuring it out sooner. That's all." She sighed and started going through the file cabinets, shifting the conversation from herself to Carrie. "Anyway, did HR ever get back to you about Carrie's recent leaves of absence?"

"They did," I said, shoving the burner phone in my pocket for later research, then continuing to go through the rest of the desk drawers. "She *has* taken a lot of time off lately, but apparently, it's legit. She has a sister who's ill. I made a few calls, and it checked out."

"Do you think she's knowingly involved in this mess with Devon?" Layla asked over her shoulder.

"Not sure, but I'm starting to think it's a possibility." I rummaged through the bottom drawer without looking up at her. "What do you think?"

"I don't know." Layla pulled out a stack of files to go through. "I mean she could have been just like me, dazzled by Devon's charm and slick persona and none the wiser about what he was doing behind the scenes. He was a master manipulator, after all."

"True." Other than the burner phone, there was nothing in the desk, dammit. "But I still think we need to talk to her."

I stood and started going through the file cabinets while Layla went through the computer. There were lots of family documents and medical records, but nothing related to the Shepperton, Inc. financials or the mess we were dealing with. If Devon had been working his illegal deals and money laundering schemes down here, then he'd cleaned up the evidence before the accident.

Two hours later, we left and went back upstairs for dinner. We shut off the lights in the storage unit and headed back out into the hall. Layla's phone rang while she waited on me to close the overhead door and secure the storage unit again. I did my best not to listen in and give her privacy, but considering the acoustics in the place, it was impossible.

"Layla Bailey. Yes. Yes, I'll be there. Thank you."

I glanced over at her as I slid the key into my pocket. "Everything okay?"

"Yeah. That was my OB/GYN calling to confirm my appointment tomorrow." Her stomach rumbled and she brushed past me toward the stairs leading back up to ground level. "I'm starving. Let's get upstairs so we can eat."

Layla

I had a funny feeling in my stomach as I climbed the stairs. Anxiety. Like something bad was about to happen, but I didn't know what or when. I used to feel the same way when my parents were out running a con and I was left behind to wait for them. It left me unsettled and confused. There was no reason for me to feel that way now. Yes, things were crazy and messy at the moment, but I was a different person than I'd been back then. No longer a scared kid, I was a grown woman, capable of handling whatever life threw at me.

And yes, sleeping with Drake hadn't exactly been part of my planned agenda, but I wouldn't have traded that night with him in our tent this past weekend for anything in the world. What we had might be temporary, but that didn't mean it was any less real or precious, right?

We reached the top of the stairs and exited the basement storage area. Drake sidled around me to head for the condo entrance while I lingered behind a moment to put my phone back in the bag. There was a chilly breeze tonight and goosebumps rose on my arms. I'd just zipped up my bag and started toward where Drake was waiting for me on the sidewalk, when an arm wrapped around me from behind and pulled me back into the shadows.

I screamed fast before a hand clamped tight over my mouth, praying it was enough to get Drake's attention. Fear and adrenaline pounded through my head, quickening my pulse and blurring my thoughts. I had learned a long time ago how to take care of myself in a scuffle—one of the few advantages of growing up the way I had—and I reacted on autopilot by stomping on my abductor's instep, then jabbing my elbow into their gut when they doubled over in pain. A muffled growl echoed, definitely male. I swiveled in his loosened grip and faced my abductor, hoping to ID him, but it was impossible because of the ski mask he wore. Damn. I thrust the heel of my hand upward where I hoped his nose would be. A sickening crack of bone sounded, followed by another howl of pain. Finally, I jammed my knee hard into the assailant's groin, knocking the man to his knees. Out of the corner of my eye, I spotted Drake, tussling with a second man. Drake landed several hard punches to his assailant's face and torso, sending the guy reeling backward toward the van idling nearby. Before I could catch my breath, the attacker I'd kneed in the balls managed to clamber to his feet and take off toward the waiting vehicle. The second man joined him and they tore out of the parking lot in a squeal of tires seconds later.

Out of breath and shocked, I bent over to rest my hands on my thighs while Drake chased after the van, trying in vain to get a license number.

"Shit!" he shouted, halting a short distance away before turning back to rush to my side. "Are you all right?"

I nodded, leaning on his solid forearm for support as he led me into the condo and sat me down on the sofa. "Who were those people?"

"No idea." He rushed back to close and lock the condo door behind us, then crouched in front of me, running his hands over me as if to assure himself I was still in one piece. "But I swear to God if I get my hands on them again, they'll regret ever coming after you like that." Once he'd checked me over from head to toe, he slumped down on the sofa next to me and ran a shaky hand through his hair, his cheeks flushed and his eyes glittering with anger and affront. Drake took several deep breaths, the tension quivering through his muscled body eventually dissipating. Finally, he looked over at me. "Where'd you learn to fight like that?"

I hesitated, then decided to let him in a little more. After all, he kind of deserved some honesty from me after the way he'd defended me tonight. I wasn't used to people fighting for me like that and it touched me more than I wanted to admit. "I got picked on a lot as a kid. Learning how to fight for myself made life easier."

Drake watched me closely for a moment, then cupped my cheek and leaned in and kissed me sweetly. "I'm glad you're okay. And no one's going to pick on you anymore. Not while I'm around. I'll take them out for you."

"Thanks." I kissed him back, the unexpected sting of tears prickling the back of my eyes before I forced them away. Must be the pregnancy hormones or leftover adrenaline or something. Had to be. I wasn't a crier. And I wasn't getting overly attached to Drake Shepperton either, no matter how my traitorous heart might be racing for him right now. Thankfully, my stomach growled again, saving me from answering any more awkward questions. "Dinner?"

"In a bit." He kissed me once more, fast, then stood, pulling me up beside him. "First we need to call the police and report what happened."

I tensed. Police weren't exactly welcome in my book, not after how I'd grown up with my parents. I'd already had to overcome my reluctance to turn to them when I'd first tried to report the break-ins and things after Devon's accident. Their frosty reception then, and again after the vandalism of my car, made me even less willing to trust them now. "Are you sure we need to get them involved?" I rubbed my arms briskly, feeling a sudden chill at his confused frown. "I mean, they weren't receptive to me before about what happened. And no real harm was done tonight. You didn't even get a license plate number or anything, did you?"

Drake's frown deepened and he placed his hands on my shoulders. "No, the van was moving too fast, and it was dark. The building has security cameras, but who knows how much they caught? We still need to make a record of this. Someone tried to kidnap you. I won't stand around and let it happen again. Even if the police can't do anything tonight, I want it on file so that if someone tries to get to you again, we have a paper trail for the future." I opened my mouth to protest further, but he held up a hand. "Sorry. It's not up for debate."

I sighed, my shoulders sagging. Hard as it was to face law enforcement again, I needed to do this. Drake wouldn't always be around to protect me. I had to be proactive about this, whether the cops would or could do much or not. "Okay."

He dialed in to the desk sergeant on duty and relayed the information about the attack, then hung up, grim-faced. "They're sending officers over now to take our statements and investigate the area. After that's done, I'll make you some dinner."

Nodding, I sat down on the sofa again, covering my face with both hands. "Thank you."

"Nothing to thank me for." He crouched in front of me and stroked my hair back away from my face. "We're in this together." When I finally looked at him, he grinned. "Speaking of together, I can take you to your doctor's appointment tomorrow too, if you want."

"Really?" I scrunched my nose. "You'd do that?"

"Of course." He took my hands and warmed them in his larger ones. "If you want me to."

Honestly, I hadn't really thought about it, but after the attack tonight, I'd feel safer having Drake by my side. "I would. I'd like that a lot, actually."

TWELVE
LAYLA

The following afternoon, I sat in the waiting room to see my doctor. Drake was beside me, as promised, thumbing through a celebrity tabloid magazine with a look most people reserved for finding something foul stuck to the bottom of their shoe.

"Do people actually pay money to read this crap?" he asked, his tone disdainful.

"Yep." I chuckled.

He shook his head and tossed the thing aside, picking up a months-old copy of a nature magazine instead. "Now this is more my speed."

"Agreed." I smiled, then looked over as the nurse came out to call me back. "That's me. See you in a bit."

Drake looked up at me. "Want me to go back with you?"

"No. I'm fine. You stay here." The look of relief on his face nearly made me laugh out loud. "I won't be long."

"Okay." He sat back in his chair and paged through an issue devoted to conservation efforts in Zimbabwe. "I'll be here."

I followed the nurse back to an exam room, got weighed and my blood pressure taken, then took a seat on the paper-covered table to wait. At least I wasn't due for another vaginal exam today. Just a check-up and an abdominal ultrasound to see if the baby's heartbeat was present and to get an accurate due date. I was pretty sure I knew how far along I was, but I wanted confirmation.

"It's nice that the baby's father came with you today. Are you sure you don't want him to come back with you to see the baby for the first time?" the nurse said from the counter against the wall where she was entering my vitals into the computer.

"What?" Startled, I snapped my attention to the woman. "Oh, he's not the father."

After the nurse left, I exhaled slowly, rethinking my decision to have Drake come with me today. Last night it had seemed like a good idea, with the attack and all, but now…ugh. Maybe I shouldn't get so worked up about it. I didn't care what people thought and I really did feel safer having Drake there with me, in case those guys from last night decided to try and abduct me again. I could take care of myself, but it was nice to know he had my back too. Especially since the police had turned out to be as unhelpful as I'd feared. They'd filed their report and looked around the parking lot, taking pictures of the skid marks from the van's tires and stuff, but again, they hadn't had much to offer as far as assurances went. They didn't think it was likely that they'd be able to find the van, and there wasn't much they could do to track down the men. When Drake had told them about his brother's accident and about the previous break-ins I'd reported and how we thought they might all be related, the cops nodded and said they'd make a note of it in the file, then left. So yeah. I wasn't holding my breath for much progress there.

Finally, a knock sounded on the door and Dr. Irbani entered, an ever-present smile on her pretty face. "Layla, so good to see you today. How's everything? Any problems with your pregnancy so far?"

"No, not really." I'd always liked the older Indian woman and felt comfortable telling her most anything about my health or body. I mentioned a couple episodes of morning sickness and the occasional abdominal cramp, but confirmed that there had been no bleeding. "I'll be glad to get a firm due date today though, so I can start planning ahead."

"Agreed." Dr. Irbani continued the exam while we chatted about the weather and life in general. Finally, the doctor had me lie back on the exam table and pull up the hem of my sweater. "This gel will feel cold and you'll feel some pressure, but you shouldn't experience any other discomfort during the ultrasound. Ready?"

"Ready," I said. The doctor lowered the lights in the room, then pulled up a stool beside the table and wheeled the ultrasound machine in front of her. The gel was icy on my skin, but that was soon forgotten as grainy images filled the screen beside me, and I got my first look at my baby. The steady *koosh-koosh-koosh* of the baby's heartbeat filled the air, bringing tears to my eyes. The doctor pointed out a head and tiny limbs, though it was hard for me to make out any clear details. My heart was full, and my head was swimming. While I'd loved my baby since I'd first discovered I was pregnant, seeing my little one onscreen for the first time brought it all home in a new and real way. I just lay there and marveled at it all. "Wow."

"Wow is right," Dr. Irbani said, grinning at me before refocusing on the computer screen. "All the measurements look normal for this stage of gestation and I'd say based on the crown-rump length, we're right on track at ten weeks. That would put your due date at around October 31 , give or take a week either way."

"A Halloween baby." I struggled to keep the wonder from my voice and failed miserably. "Halloween is my favorite holiday."

"Now you'll have one more reason to love it." Dr. Irbani captured a few stills and printed them out for me to keep then finished up the ultrasound. She was just about to stop when something onscreen must have caught her eye, based on the way she frowned and leaned in closer.

"What?" I asked, concern flooding my system. "Is something wrong?"

"No. Not wrong." Dr. Irbani squirted more gel on Layla's stomach and shifted the placement of the probe on my abdomen, trying to get a different angle. The rush of the baby's heartbeat seemed to grow louder, echoing through the room. The doctor gave a low whistle, then sat back to click several keys on the keyboard in front of her, snapping more photos and recording more measurements. "I'm afraid I have some news for you, Ms. Bailey."

Fear, worse than anything I'd experienced before, froze the blood in my veins. Worse than the day my parents had been arrested. Worse than the day I'd testified against them in court and essentially put them away for life. Worse than the day of Devon's accident or even the attack last night. I swallowed hard and stared at Dr. Irbani as I promised myself that whatever it was, as long as my baby would be okay, I'd deal with it. "What is it?"

The doctor shut off the ultrasound machine and turned up the lights once more, taking off her gloves and tossing them in a biohazard bin nearby before washing her hands. The suspense was killing me and if Dr. Irbani didn't spit out the news soon, I might just shake the woman silly to get it out of her.

Finally, the doctor took a seat on her stool again and wheeled over to face me, handing me the extra photos from the ultrasound. I looked at them but couldn't really understand what I was seeing. I'd had a hard enough time making out anything in the first ones. With my blood pounding in my ears and my heart racing, it was impossible now.

"Please tell me what's wrong," I said, my stomach cramping from anxiety. "I can't tell what's what in these."

"Nothing's wrong, Ms. Bailey." The doctor patted my knee and smiled. "Your baby's fine. Both of them."

It took a moment for my brain to register that information through the fog of worry. When I did, I felt completely poleaxed. Perhaps I should have expected it, knowing about Devon and Drake, but still. "Both?"

"Yep." Dr. Irbani gave a joyful laugh. "Congratulations, Ms. Bailey, you're having twins."

Drake

I checked my watch again, then gazed out the windows across from me. It felt like I'd been waiting out here forever, but in reality, it had probably only been half an hour. I should have insisted on going back there with Layla. I didn't like being separated from her after last night.

Each time a door opened from the area where the offices were located, I started to get up, hoping it was Layla. But each time I'd been disappointed. I'd read through every decent magazine in the place and even a few of those stupid tabloid ones too. I was just about ready to get up and go to the desk to check and see what was taking so long back there when Layla finally emerged back into the waiting room, her checkout paperwork in hand and her face far too pale for my liking.

"What?" I asked, rushing to her side and taking her icy fingers in mine. "What's wrong?"

She didn't answer, just walked past me out the door and into the sunny parking lot. I cursed under my breath and followed her outside, mentally calling my dead brother every name in the book for leaving Layla in this situation, to deal with all of this all alone.

We walked to the car, and I opened the door for her, helping her inside before jogging around to climb in behind the wheel of my company SUV. The suspense became too much, though, and I couldn't wait any longer to ask. "Please just tell me that there's nothing wrong with the baby."

"Huh?" She looked up at me, frowning, as if just then realizing I was there. "No, the baby's fine. They're *both* fine."

I blinked at her a moment, taking that in. "Both?"

Her dazed expression slowly gave way to uncertainty. "I'm having twins."

"That's…" I was about to say "great," or maybe "wonderful," or "congratulations." But the look on her face stopped me. Based on her pale complexion and wide eyes, Layla was terrified. I gathered her into my arms instead and held her as closely as possible given the awkwardness of our position in the vehicle. "Hey, it's going to be okay. I promise." I kissed the top of her head, rocking her slowly until she relaxed against me. "We'll figure it all out. Together. Partners, right?"

She sniffled and sat back; her dark brows knit as she stared down at her hands in her lap. "This is beyond helping me with the mess Devon left behind. You don't have to—"

"Shh." I placed a finger over her lips to stop her. "Don't be ridiculous. Of course I'll help you through this. Whatever you need. I might not know much about babies and raising kids, but I can learn. You can count on me, Layla. I won't let you down."

Layla didn't say much after that and the mood in the car turned somber. I pulled out of the parking lot and headed back toward the condo, searching for some way to brighten her mood. Yes, twins would be more work, but they could also mean twice the joy. And sure, I was a bit partial, being a twin myself, but that didn't pop the bubble of excitement welling inside me.

As we pulled up to a red light, I looked over and saw a local baby superstore up ahead on the right. Maybe buying a few new things for the babies would brighten her mood.

When I pulled up to the front of the store, Layla gave me a confused stare. "Why are we here?"

I pulled into a parking spot and cut the engine. "Thought maybe we could get a few things to celebrate."

"Oh, I don't know." Layla folded her paperwork and stuck it in her bag. "I haven't really figured out a budget yet for how much I can afford to spend."

"My treat." I winked at her and opened my car door. "Seriously. Let Uncle Drake spoil the kids a little bit."

She chuckled at that and my day brightened. "Uncle Drake, huh?"

"Yep." I walked around to open her door for her. "And after we go shopping, I'm taking you back to the condo and cooking you one of my special dishes."

"Special?" Layla gave me a side glance. "Like what?"

"How about candied salmon and rice?" I took her hand as we walked toward the store.

"Oh! I do love salmon," she said, resting her head on my shoulder, smiling at last. "Sounds good."

"It does, doesn't it?" I smiled myself, kissing the top of her head.

THIRTEEN

DRAKE

The next day, I was back at my desk, scowling down at the report I'd received earlier that morning from Zach Walker. He'd sent it over in an email with the message *You're not going to like this* attached. Not only did it confirm all of my worst fears about my brother's crash, it brought up new doubts and questions as well.

As I'd started to suspect, it turned out Devon's accident wasn't an accident at all. The findings from the police report, along with a detailed reconstruction done at the scene, proved that my brother's vehicle had been deliberately run off the road. From the angle of the tire tracks and the data downloaded from the vehicle's black box, the speed and trajectory of the impact sent him careening head-on into a tree. Add in the fact Devon never wore his seatbelt and he'd been a broken neck waiting to happen.

I shook my head and scrubbed a hand over my face.

Shit. Just shit.

If I had a nickel for every time growing up I'd warned my brother to buckle up…

I sighed and shook my head, staring down at the report again. Not that it would have mattered. Devon never listened to anyone but himself. Another Shepperton family trait. One that I had worked hard to overcome in myself through my military training. In the military, and most especially in a special ops unit, not working with your team or disobeying orders could mean the difference between life and death.

Seemed my brother had learned that lesson the hard way.

Zach had included a note pointing out that while an outside driver had definitely caused the crash, it was actually Devon's choice not to wear his seatbelt that had ended his life. With that model of car and the type of crash, the airbags probably would have saved him. But the lack of a seatbelt put his body in the wrong position when the airbags deployed, and his neck snapped as a result.

Setting the report aside, I moved on to the stack of financial reports I'd requested from accounting a few days prior, hoping for a distraction from the mess of my brother's death. But no respite was in sight, given that the financials were an even bigger red flag that foul play was involved in Devon's demise.

An odd mix of anticipation and dread had me on my feet, reports in hand, as I headed out of my office toward the accounting department. I needed to talk to Jameson again. Of all the people involved in the financial aspects of the Shepperton Foundation—other than Layla—Jameson was the one I was most willing to trust. Jameson had never authorized any grants.

I took the elevator down several floors, then made a beeline for Jameson's office door. The older man was working at his desk when I knocked and walked in, shutting the door behind me for privacy.

"Mr. Shepperton," Jameson said, starting to get up. "What can I help you with?"

"We need to discuss these reports," I said, gesturing for Jameson to stay seated while I took a chair in front of the man's desk and spread the financial paperwork in my hand out on the desktop before us. "There are a bunch of fishy transactions on here, mainly connected to how the grant money was disbursed, and I think we need an immediate full and fiduciary audit into the foundation."

At first, Jameson just blinked at me, his face blank. Then, slowly, the man's expression morphed from wary to relieved. "Oh, thank goodness. I was hoping you'd say that. Honestly, I've had my suspicions for a while now about how the money was being handled, but I hadn't been authorized to really look into it until now. Thank you."

"Don't thank me yet," I said, sitting back. "It's going to be a massive amount of work and we need to keep it under wraps for now until we have a better idea of exactly who's involved in the misdeeds."

"Understood, sir." Jameson nodded. "May I be frank with you?"

"Please."

"I hate to say it, sir, but I'd be very surprised if your brother wasn't involved, at least in some fashion."

"Why is that?" I asked, doing my best to hide the fact that I felt the same way. I wanted to get a picture of the situation from Jameson's perspective, without influencing it in any way.

"Well, there's just been some very odd things happening in those accounts over the last several years." Jameson folded his hands atop the papers on his desk, his brows drawing together above his wire-rimmed glasses. "I didn't realize the extent of them all until I became CFO and had access to that information. Starting with the dismissal of many of the staff dealing with the financials and the executive director for the Shepperton Foundation. All of these were good, competent people who shouldn't have been let go, in my opinion. There was no reason for it, not that I'm aware of anyway. And because of their abrupt dismissals, in violation of HR procedures and practices, they each received substantial severance packages as well. The reason stated publicly for their leaving was that job cuts were needed to save money. But the payment of those large sums in severance after the fact suggests that saving money wasn't a factor at all. At least not in the way the press releases implied."

"Hmm." I steepled my fingers and tapped them against my lips, my frown deepening. "So, it was more like these people were being paid off to keep quiet?"

"Exactly." Jameson smiled. "Given the routineness of severance packages being paid to ousted execs these days, no one really thought twice about it at the time, though. In fact, it wasn't until Ms. Bailey asked me to look into the grant money that I began to wonder about those golden-parachute payments. That's when I did a little digging on my own and didn't like what I found. Then, of course, there was your brother's accident. I put two and two together, but was still hoping that somehow, I might be wrong." Jameson shuddered, his pale face going even whiter. "If these payments and the other financial missteps had something to do with his death, that would be very distressing indeed."

"Indeed," I repeated then sat forward. "Right. Well, I think you and I are on the same page for now. My brother was nothing if not shifty, and it seems like an operation of this scale couldn't have started anywhere other than at the top." I'd heard of so many misdeeds over the years, saying such awful things about my brother didn't even faze me anymore. Which was sad, if I'd had time to think about it. "So, if Devon was involved in money laundering through the Shepperton Foundation, why? From what I've seen so far, Shepperton, Inc. is very successful at the moment and that was trickling down to the foundation too."

"Yes," Jameson said. "Things have been going well for the company. That makes me suspect that your brother was doing this on behalf of someone else. I've got a few hunches about who, but I haven't dug any deeper to confirm those suspicions so I don't want to say anything yet."

"Nothing concrete then?" I asked.

"No. Not yet."

"Okay." I stood to pace the room. I did my best thinking while moving. "Go ahead and start looking deeper into whatever you think is relevant. I'll wait until you complete your investigation before I talk to the company's legal counsel. We want to make sure our ducks are in a row before we bring in the big guns." I stopped before the older man's bookcase and stared at the old ledgers stored there. "Also, how much do you know about Carrie Bartlett?"

Jameson gave me a surprised look. "Not much. Just that she was an associate who reported to your brother. Why?"

"They were also sleeping together." I took a deep breath. "I think she might be in on all this too. If you find out during your investigation that she's authorized anything—grant money, travel expenditures, whatever—in the last year or so, I want to know about it. And while I think it's likely that Devon was the one coordinating all of this, we shouldn't ignore other possibilities. She might have been doing it under the guise of my brother's consent, so be sure to check the signatures on his deals to makes sure it's actually Devon's and not hers signing on his behalf. You recognize the difference between the two handwritings?"

"Yes, sir." Jameson gave a curt nod. "I've seen them both and can tell them apart. I'll be sure to look into Ms. Bartlett as well."

"Good." I headed for the door, then turned back. "The days ahead are likely to be the roughest in Shepperton, Inc. history, Jameson. Are you prepared to handle that?"

"I am, sir," Jameson said, squaring his slender shoulders beneath his tweed sport coat. "I've worked for this company in one capacity or another since I was in college. I love Shepperton, Inc. as if it's my own. And though it may be rough, these things must be rooted out for the greater good. Better to do it now and deal with it, so we don't disrupt operations any further and put more people's livelihoods at risk."

FOURTEEN

DRAKE

Over dinner that night, I updated Layla on the Zach's report about the accident and my later conversation with Jameson. I hated the fact that the upsetting news might ruin her appetite, but I knew I needed to let her know what was happening.

"I'm sorry if that news upsets you," I said, wincing at her too-pale complexion and the dark circles under her eyes. "But I think it's important that you know what we're dealing with here, and how far these people are willing to go. After that attack in the parking lot the other night, we have to consider the fact that the same people who ran Devon off the road are now coming after you."

"Jesus." She pushed her half-eaten plate of salad aside, then just stared blankly at her water glass. "Even suspecting ahead of time that Devon had been killed, having it confirmed is just…wow."

"I know." I reached over and took her hand, my pulse thundering in my ears. "I feel the same way. My brother and I were not close, but knowing his accident wasn't an accident at all and that he was murdered?" I swallowed hard against the burn in the back of my throat. "That just takes all this to a whole other level."

Crimson dotted her white cheeks, and she squeezed my fingers tighter between her icy ones, placing her free hand atop her stomach. "So, you think these people are after me now too?"

"I don't know. But I think we have to consider all possibilities. Maybe Devon warned them you were asking questions; maybe they think you're in a position to uncover too much now that Devon's not around to keep you distracted…or maybe they have some other motive we haven't figured out yet. Given the fact you two were involved personally as well for a time, it could be that whoever did this might assume you knew about my brother's illicit activities and might go to the authorities with that information."

She shook her head, trembling beneath my touch. All my protective instincts went haywire, urging me to hold her close and never let her go, but I couldn't do that. Not yet. Not until this mess was over with, at least. Maybe not ever, since I'd be leaving soon and Layla deserved someone who would stay at her side forever.

"But I don't know anything. Not really," she said, her voice quiet.

"I know that, but they don't." I rubbed her chilled hand with mine, hoping to convey some warmth and strength to her, since that was all I had to give at the moment. "For all we know, whoever Devon was laundering that money for is still waiting on more payments. If that's true, they might even think you can get the funds for them. That could explain why they tried to abduct you. If they had only wanted to silence you, they wouldn't have needed to bring a van to drag you away."

"But that's crazy!" she cried, her breath hitching and her eyes bright with unshed tears. "What good could I do for them? Devon was the one who was willing to cooperate with them, and they killed him in the end. Why would they do that if he was their best way to get their money?

And what would they do to me to try to force me to give it to them? Oh, God, Drake. This is all such a mess. What if they come after me again? I'm not scared for myself, but what about my babies?"

I was out of my seat in a moment, forgetting my vows to keep the distance, forgetting my promise not to touch her since I might not be around much longer, forgetting everything except the burning need to hold her and comfort her and assure her that I would do anything in my power to keep her and the babies safe. "I won't let them get to you. I promise. I won't let them touch you or the babies. Understand?"

I whispered the words against the top of her head, and she nodded beneath my chin, her hands clasping my sides tightly. We stayed that way for a long moment, until she sighed and relaxed against me and I finally let her go before I couldn't anymore. We sat back down, and I held her hand again, just because it felt so good to touch her.

"So, after I went over the accident investigation report, I went down and talked to the CFO. He's going to look deeper into the issues we discovered. He'd had some suspicions of his own about Devon mishandling funds, so he's already got some leads he's looking into." I laced our fingers together once more, my thumb rubbing tiny circles over the racing pulse point in her wrist to help calm her. "I trust him. He'll find whatever's hidden there, I'm sure, but I warned him that things are going to get rough over the next few weeks, PR-wise."

"Agreed." Her tense shoulders slumped, and she stared down at the tabletop. "All of this mess will likely delay the sale of Shepperton, Inc. too. Which means you'll be in Dallas longer than you planned."

"True." A few weeks ago, that idea would have made me restless and jumpy. Now all I cared about was keeping the beautiful woman across from me safe, happy, and healthy for as long as I could. In fact, a few more weeks here with her sounded like heaven on earth. My heart squeezed and warmth spread through my torso. Not that I'd tell her that. She had enough to deal with right now without my feelings on top of it. We'd both started this thing between us knowing it was only temporary, and I shouldn't rock the boat, no matter how love might have capsized my good intentions already. "But that doesn't matter to me." She looked up and we locked eyes, the heat in her gaze matching the fire inside me for her. "All that matters is you and me and what we're doing here, together."

"Together," she whispered, leaning across the table to kiss me.

"Together," I said against her lips. Then there was just her and me and the crazy storm of things she made me feel, whether I should or not.

FIFTEEN

LAYLA

I checked my appearance in the living room mirror for the umpteenth time. The amethyst-colored dress was new and when I'd bought it a few weeks prior for the gala tonight, it had fit perfectly. Now, though, the satin and chiffon pulled too tight at the waist, and it felt like my ever-increasing bosom was going to burst through the bodice. I'd expected to have to revamp my wardrobe at some point during the pregnancy, just not this soon.

I was still fiddling with my full skirt when Drake walked in, looking devastatingly handsome in his tux. Darn it. Men had it so easy with formalwear and didn't even know or appreciate it. All they had to do was put on the same black suit and bow tie with a white shirt and they were ready to go.

"Stop fidgeting," he said, coming up behind me and wrapping his arms around my middle, giving me a gentle squeeze as he kissed one of my bare shoulders. The halter neckline left me feeling a bit exposed thanks to my growing bust size, but feeling the heat of Drake against my bare skin was one advantage of my outfit, I supposed. He met my gaze in the mirror and smiled, his teeth even and white against his tanned complexion. "You look beautiful."

"Thank you," I said, warmth prickling my cheeks as joy fizzed inside me like champagne. For the first time in a long time, I felt safe and protected, and I had Drake to thank for that. No matter how things turned out between us when this was all over, I would always be grateful to him. He leaned in to nuzzle the nape of my neck and I couldn't suppress a shiver of delight at the magical chemistry between us. I'd never felt anything like it, not even with Devon. If I wasn't careful, my "like" for him could tumble right over into something more—something devastating. Before I completely melted into his arms, I forced myself to pull away and turned to straighten his slightly crooked bowtie. "And you look very nice yourself, sir."

"'Sir,' huh?" He quirked one dark brow at me. "Are you trying to get me all hot and bothered, *miss*? Because if so, mission accomplished."

"Yeah?" I flashed a slow grin, savoring the rising desire in his eyes. Even as stressed as I was by everything, he could still make me forget it all with one sexy look. Amazing.

"Oh yeah." He pulled me close again, his fingers stroking my sides through the silky material of my dress. "Maybe we should just skip this gala altogether and stay home tonight. I'm sure we could find something here to enjoy just as much."

"Hmm." I slid my arms around his neck and rose on tiptoe to kiss him fast before moving away. "I wish we could, but I need to be there tonight. I was on the planning committee for this event, and the foundation has been a sponsor for years. This annual gala raises a huge amount for kids with Loorer's Disease. It's one of my passion projects, and I love supporting it."

He sighed and tried to pull me back against him once more. "I thought *I* was your passion project?"

I swatted his hands away and checked my chignon once more before heading for the foyer to grab my cashmere wrap. "You are. In a different way. You can stay home if you want, but I'm going."

Drake shook his head and grabbed his keys off the side table by the door. "No. If you're going, I'm going too. After what happened the other night in the parking lot, I'm not letting you out of my sight."

Drake

The gala was just as lavish as I had expected. It was just the kind of thing my family would have loved. My parents had prided themselves on attending all of the biggest and best shindigs this side of the Mississippi, and Devon loved showing off his wealth and privilege in the most ostentatious way possible. I was the only odd duck out, preferring quiet get-togethers with friends, where people could actually talk and relax. The gala tonight was not one of those.

Above our heads, the ceiling of the enormous event space was covered with diaphanous clear and white balloons that reflected the blue and green spotlights directed at us, giving the whole room a sort of underwater feel. A sea of white-linen-covered tables flowed out across the ballroom floor, and silverware and crystal sparkled from the tabletops. At the center of each round table were elegant centerpieces of white roses and lilies in tall crystal vases. Near the front of the space was a small stage and a flat screen monitor. In front of that a dancefloor had been set up and a small orchestra played off to the side of the space, old standards and a few new ballads also, to keep things interesting.

It all reeked of money and power and pretension, and I was bored out of my mind.

The only thing that kept the night interesting was tracking Layla's movements around the room. From the moment we'd entered the party, she'd gone off to mix and mingle and schmooze. I'd snagged a glass of champagne from a passing waiter and stayed near the sidelines, keeping an eye on her. I hadn't been kidding earlier. I was still worried about someone trying to take her again, especially after my meeting with Jameson the other day and our decision to dig deeper into the death of my brother. Whoever had run my brother's car off the road had been desperate, and desperation didn't just go away. No. The people whose money my brother had been laundering were still out there. In all likelihood, they still wanted their funds—and they could no longer appeal to Devon for them. If they thought that Layla was their best shot, they wouldn't stop until they had her in their custody, or until I got to them first.

Either way, Layla wasn't going to disappear on me again.

I sipped my champagne, watching her over the rim of my glass as several fundraiser attendees sidled past me. I stepped back to allow them to pass, only to bump arms with someone else.

"Excuse me," I said, glancing over my shoulder at the older, white-haired man behind me.

"No problem," the older man said, his blue gaze narrowed. "Aren't you Drake Shepperton?"

Damn. I'd hoped to lie low tonight and observe people to see if anyone was acting suspicious, but that wasn't to be, apparently. I plastered on my most polite smile and turned to shake hands with the man. This fundraiser was important to Layla, which made it important to me too. I had no idea who the hell this man was, but I wasn't about to do anything to offend him and maybe put the foundation in a negative light. I swallowed hard against the lump of dread in my throat and said, "Yes. Drake Shepperton, at your service. And you are?"

"Baron Bexler," the man said, his grip more energetic than necessary. Only in Texas would you see a guy in a tux wearing a tie covered with longhorn skulls. I downed the rest of my champagne in one gulp. If the older man noticed anything odd, he didn't show it, just grinned widely as he nearly dislocated my shoulder with his over-enthusiastic greeting. "Such an honor, sir. Really. Thank you for your service. And I'm so sorry about your brother. Too bad. Devon was quite a guy."

"Yeah." I set my empty glass aside and took another from the waiter walking by. It was going to be a long evening. I checked to make sure Layla was still talking with the same group of people near the stage, then focused on Bexler again. "So, what business are you in, Mr. Bexler?"

"Baron, please," the guy said, pointing to his tie. "And beef, if you couldn't already tell. Got the largest ranch in the county, with almost a million acres and twice as many longhorns. Your brother loved to come out on the weekends and enjoy my facilities. Love to have you come out some time too, Drake. Besides the mansion, we've got golf, swimming, tennis. Even a shooting range."

"Great." I took another swig of champagne, feeling this conversation slowly draining away my will to live. I saw Layla excuse herself from one group and move on to the next, this time a bit closer to the exit sign along the wall. If I moved fast, I might be able to pull her away and out onto the dancefloor. But then Bexler said something that got my attention.

"Honestly, I was trying to convince your brother to let me buy Shepperton, Inc. Per my financial advisor's counsel, I've been trying to diversify my holdings and I thought—"

"You want to buy my company?" I said, my eyes widening a bit. I'd been searching for weeks for someone to take the company off my hands, but I'd never checked with local cattlemen. Maybe this evening wouldn't be a total bust for me after all. "Let's sit down and discuss it some more, shall we?"

We walked to a nearby table to talk and I was soon knee-deep in conversations about balance sheets and year projections and future visions for the company. Something I never would have imagined myself doing just a few months prior, but such was my life now. At least until this mess was settled. I didn't know whether to be pleased with myself or horrified that I actually knew the answers to all of Bexler's questions—but at least that helped move the conversation along. Bexler had a good head for business, beneath all those layers of longhorn-imprinted silk, and we communicated well together, both straight talkers without a lot of BS mixed in to confuse things.

When I finally came up for air, I glanced toward the exit again, but didn't see Layla. Frowning, I checked the groups of people nearby, but saw no sign of that breathtaking purple dress of hers. I pushed to my feet to better scan the area. She wouldn't leave without telling me. She had to be here somewhere. Was she in the bathroom? How long had she been gone? I couldn't be sure.

"So, should we schedule an appointment at your office, to discuss this formally?" Bexler asked.

I looked down at the guy, too distracted now to think about my schedule. "Uh, yes. Sure. Have your assistant call my secretary in the morning." I scribbled down the number on a napkin for Bexler. "If you'll excuse me, I need to locate someone."

I took off without waiting for Bexler's response. Weaving through the throngs of designer-clad people, I vaguely responded to the greetings of attendees as I passed, concentrating only on finding Layla. When I stopped one of the waiters to ask if he'd seen her, the guy pointed toward the exit where I had last seen her, saying she went outside, probably to get some fresh air or something.

Or something?

Gut tight and pulse pounding, I shoved forward toward the green glowing sign above the door, barely noticing the people I passed, not caring if I was rude or not. Layla's safety was all that mattered now. Her and the twins. I would not fail them. Not again. I pushed outside and into the warm Texas night, the dark sky above sparkling with stars as far as the eye could see, but I didn't care about any of it. All I cared about was finding Layla.

The sound of a scuffle nearby made me whip my head around in time to see a flash of deep purple. Layla's dress. I took off at a run toward the end of the line of cars nearby and spotted one of her strappy shoes lying on the pavement.

Oh God. OhGodOhGodOhGod.

There was another sound, a muffled scream followed by a deep grunt.

Adrenaline sizzling through my veins, I quickened my steps, sprinting in the direction of the sound, and happened upon a large guy dressed in all black, his beefy arms wrapped tight around Layla while he held a white cloth over her mouth with one hand. She was twisting her head from side to side, making it harder for her attacker to hold the cloth in place. I went into full SEAL mode in zero seconds flat.

I charged the guy, who was concentrating so hard on keeping Layla contained that he didn't see me approach, and rammed him hard with my full body weight, knocking the guy back a few steps and freeing Layla from his grasp.

"Stay the fuck away from her, asshole!" I shouted, my breath tight in my chest and my body tensed and ready for a fight. "I swear to God if you hurt one hair on her head, I will kill you."

The thug came at me, and I lowered my head, barreling into the guy's middle with my skull and knocking the wind out of my opponent. The guy was big and sturdy and landed a few punches to my face and torso, but I knew how to fight hard and dirty and didn't hesitate to use all my skills to hit Layla's attacker where it hurt the most—gut, groin, voice box. Soon, the brawl caught the attention of the valets out front and their shouts and footsteps had the thug jumping into a waiting van before I could get him down on the ground to rip that mask off his face and identify the bastard.

Within seconds, they disappeared into the night. I was left out of breath and doubled over, resting my hands on my knees as I sucked in a few painful gulps of oxygen. Fucker cracked at least two ribs, by my estimation, but I was certain my attacker would be walking funny for days.

Layla was at my side, trembling from head to toe, and running her hands over my back frantically like I might expire on her at any second. "Are you okay?"

"I'm fine," I said gruffly, pulling her against me, needing to see for myself that she wasn't hurt. "I'm sorry. I'm so sorry."

"For what?" she said against my chest.

"For letting that asshole get his hands on you. I should've kept better watch. I should've protected you." I kept kissing the top of her head, rubbing her arms, her back, anywhere I could reach, to convince myself she was here, she was all right. "This is my fault."

"Stop it." She shook her head, then peered up at me, her cheeks pale and her eyes sparkling. "This isn't your fault. If anything, it's mine. I dragged you into this mess. And you *did* protect me. That guy's gone now, and I'm fine."

I scowled and stepped back from her, holding her at arms' length to look her up and down. Her hair had fallen out of its neat bun and one side of her dress was torn and if I ever got my hands on that fucker again, I was going to take him out. Permanently. I took a deep breath to calm the rage threatening to overtake me, and instead turned to the two young valets who were standing off to the side of them, looking uncertain. "Call the police and tell them there's been an attack in the parking lot." The guys ran off back toward the building and I pulled Layla close again, saying, "Once we give them a report, we're going to the ER to get you checked out. I'm not taking any more chances with you or the twins."

SIXTEEN

LAYLA

"Any nausea, vomiting, or lightheadedness?" the ER doc asked while examining me. "Can you tell me how many fingers I'm holding up?"

"Two," I said, getting more annoyed by the second. I was all for making sure the babies were fine after the attack in the parking lot, but the fact that Drake was hovering around me now like a nervous mother hen bothered me more than anything. Of course, the fullness in my chest that signaled a good cry was imminent as soon as we were out of this place didn't help either. I wasn't a crier. Never had been. Growing up, standing around whining about something—no matter how terrible or unjust—was a quick way to get smacked. I'd learned early and well to suck it up and get on with it. As a result, it was deeply embarrassing to me whenever I found myself unable to hold back tears—especially in front of someone else. Even if all I wanted to do at present was hurl myself into Drake's arms and bury my head against his shoulder.

Nope. Not doing that. Stay strong. Stay ready. Stay alert.

The pep talk going on inside my head only amplified the rising tension inside until I felt ready to explode.

"Well," the ER doc said, moving away to type her findings into the computer against the wall. "I'd say both you and the babies came through the ordeal unscathed. You and your husband should be fine to go home as soon as I get your paperwork finished and your lab results back."

"He's not my husband," I snapped before I could catch myself, and heat prickled my cheeks. It wasn't the doctor's fault I was here tonight. It was stupid Devon and whatever rotten schemes he'd been up to. At the doctor's startled look, I stared down at my hands clasped protectively over my belly. "Drake is just a friend."

"A friend who's concerned about your well-being," Drake said, frowning. "Doctor, are you sure it's okay to release her? Maybe she should have a stress test or an ultrasound to make sure—"

"I'm fine, all right?" Once again, the stress inside me boiled over into misplaced rage. Drake was staring at me now like a deer in the headlights and guilt joined the roiling mess inside me, but I was on a roll and couldn't stop now. "Why the hell are you so worried about me and these babies anyway? They're not yours and you won't even be around when they're born. We're not your concern, okay? Not me and not my babies."

Drake blinked at me a second as if taking that in, dots of crimson forming on his pale cheeks. Silence stretched taut between us, and if I could have taken my words back, I would have—but it was too late. And honestly, they weren't entirely wrong either. I'd be lying if I said I hadn't been thinking about that more lately, ever since we'd slept together. I had done my best to push it out of my mind, but tonight—with the attack—all those worries had rushed back full force.

"I'm, uh, just going to run out to the nurses' station real fast to grab some instruction sheets and I'll be back in a moment to get you folks on your way. Excuse me," the doctor said, hurrying out of the room like her butt was on fire. I couldn't really blame her. As it was, I was stuck here in this room with the one man I couldn't escape. Deep in my heart, I knew that even after he was gone, Drake Shepperton would stay with me forever.

I ought to say something, but the more I tried to force words, the blanker my mind felt. Honestly, what was I going to tell him? "Sorry for putting it all out there like that, but it's the truth"? "Sorry I slept with your brother when I knew he wasn't even remotely the man for me and now I'm carrying his legacy"? "Sorry you won't stick around because you can't stick around, and I went and fell in love with you regardless"?

Yeah, none of that was going to help anything at all and I was nothing if not resilient. So I let my accusations sit there, hanging in the air between us like live grenades waiting for the final pin to be pulled.

After several tense seconds, Drake cursed under his breath and stalked away to stand in the corner with his phone in his hand, scowling down at the screen and effectively shutting me out. My heart caved in on itself a little more. His angry indifference was almost worse than his cloying concern, but I'd created this mess and now I needed to find a way to be okay with it.

Thankfully, the doctor returned a couple minutes later to go over the discharge paperwork with me. Basically, rest, eat, drink lots of fluids, call them if anything weird happened. I nodded and smiled when appropriate, anything to get this over with so I could get out of this room and away from Drake.

Except once we left the hospital, we had the car ride back to the condo. Then the stilted interactions once we went inside. Normally the place felt open and airy, but now Drake and I seemed to run into each other every time we moved, and we were constantly in each other's way.

I took a shower, then changed into my PJs and sat on the edge of the bed, too restless to sleep but too afraid of another confrontation with Drake to go back out into the living room. Anything I said now would probably just make things worse, so I sat there staring at the wall instead, berating myself for losing my temper at the hospital until a knock on my door made me look up to see Drake slumped against the doorframe.

"Look," he said, his dark brows knit as he stared down at his hands. "I'm sorry if I was crowding you tonight at the ER. That was never my intention." He sighed and met my gaze, his dark eyes full of contrition. "I just…" He shrugged. "I just kept thinking about how terrifying that attack tonight must've been for you, and I wasn't there to help and…" Drake shook his head and looked away again. "I feel like shit about that. I should've been there in time to stop it before it even started. It's my job to be there. To protect you."

I started to open my mouth and he winced, holding up a hand. "No. You were right at the hospital. I'm sorry. Those aren't my babies and you and I aren't—" He gestured between us. "Well, you know. Anyway, I can't give you what you need. And I'm sorry about that, but that's probably why we never should've gotten involved in the first place."

Hearing him say that, even though I'd been thinking the same earlier, hurt like a knife in my chest. I swallowed around the tightness in my throat and narrowed my gaze on him. "You regret sleeping with me."

It wasn't a question, but he was quick to answer anyway. "What? No. Hell no. I don't regret any of the time we've spent together, Layla. Truth is, I've loved every minute of it." Those words should have made me feel better, but instead they only made the ache inside me worse. I'd loved spending time with him too. Loved *him*, period, even if I shouldn't. Drake took a deep breath, then walked over to sit beside me on the bed, not touching me at all, his hands clasped between his knees. "Layla, you're a wonderful woman. Fun, kind, generous. Dedicated to your job and to helping others. You love astronomy almost as much as I do." At my snort, he amended, "Okay, fine, just as much as I do." He hung his head and gave a sad little laugh. "I wish we could've spent more time watching the stars together. If things were different, you're exactly the type of person I'd want to spend the rest of my life with. But our lives are too complicated now for either of us to even think about a relationship."

I considered his words, wanted to argue with them, but couldn't. He was right. I knew that deep inside, even if I hated it. I fiddled with the duvet and asked, "So, what now?"

Drake cleared his throat and straightened, clapping his hands on his thighs. "So, we keep looking into this fiasco my brother created until we find out what really happened and why he was killed, then we make sure the people involved are brought to justice. We put them away for a long time to make sure you and the babies are safe, then we both get back to our normal lives."

"And *us*?" My breath hitched a little, the corner of my eye twitching. "What do we do about this?"

I'd moved my stuff into the master bedroom with his, but that wouldn't work if we weren't sleeping together anymore. The king-sized mattress was big enough to fit four comfortably, but it would be too weird sleeping together without sleeping together.

Drake pushed to his feet and walked to the closet to grab his duffle bag. "You stay in here, and I'll move to the guest room."

"That's not fair," I said, standing too, then placing a hand on my side where the sore muscles pulled. Drake noticed, because of course he did, then pointed at the bed. I sat back down, my shoulders slumping. I was tired. More tired than I could ever remembering being, and all I wanted to do was curl up in a ball and sleep for days—but not alone. Still, I couldn't ask Drake to stay now, not after everything that had happened and what he'd just said. "You were here first. This whole place belongs to you. I should move back into the guest room."

"Hell. No." He didn't look at me as he said it, just continued to shove clothes into his bag without appearing to care that they were getting wrinkled. "You're dealing with enough. You deserve the big bed and the luxury bathroom. I'm used to cots and pit toilet latrines. Just having indoor plumbing is like being at the Ritz for me."

Despite the crappy situation, I couldn't help laughing. "I wish I'd met you first, before Devon."

He met my gaze, his own filled with heat and affection. "Me too."

We stared at each other across the span of a few feet, an ocean of yearning between us.

Finally, Drake looked away again as he emptied the dresser drawers of his socks and undies. "But things are what they are, and we need to make the best of them." Finished, he zipped up his duffle bag then slung it over his shoulder to head out the door. Halfway into the hall, he stopped and looked back at me. "We okay here?"

I nodded, feeling very not okay inside, but hiding it well. I'd had years of practice. "We're good." I even forced a smile for his benefit. "See you in the morning."

"Night," Drake said. "Sleep tight."

The door closed behind him and I lay back on the bed, staring up at the ceiling, wondering how in the world things had gone from lovely to lonely so fast.

"Mr. Bexler. It's great to hear from you," I said the next morning in the office. The prospective buyer I'd met at the gala had called first thing today. Always a positive sign of interest. I was eager to move Shepperton, Inc. off my plate, that was true, but I didn't want to lose my tactical advantage in negotiating too soon, so I played innocent. Maybe I'd learned more from my family about being a businessman than I'd given myself credit for. "What can I do for you today?"

"What you can do is sell me your company," the older man said, his Texas drawl as pronounced as it had been the previous evening. "You seemed amenable to an offer when we talked last night."

"Hmm." I sat back in my seat, doing my best to keep my mind on the conversation at hand and not the attack that had happened with Layla in the parking lot. Each time I remembered the gala, the horror I'd felt in those awful moments pushed everything else aside. The abject fear of being too late, of being helpless. The searing adrenaline as I'd rushed to save her, overpowering everything I knew about combat and disarming your adversaries. The need to protect the woman I loved at all costs.

My chest squeezed tight at the memory of our talk in the bedroom. Those words had been the hardest I'd ever had to say, telling Layla that we needed to end our tryst. I wanted her more than I wanted my next breath, but sometimes wanting wasn't enough. Ending the affair was the right decision—but that didn't mean my body was on board with it. Now, each time I closed my eyes, I'd swear I could still feel her there, could still smell her sweet floral perfume, could still taste her on my lips when I licked them.

Hell, she seemed to be closer to me now that I'd let her go than she'd ever been before when we were sleeping together, if that were possible.

Just my luck. The ghost of her will haunt me for eternity.

"Mr. Shepperton?" Bexler asked over the phone line, his tone concerned. "You still there?"

"Yes. Sorry," I said, straightening. Forcing my head back into the game and out of fantasies and fairy tales that could never be reality. I'd made my choice regarding Layla, and now I had to deal with it and move on with my life. And to accomplish that, I needed to deal with selling the company. Bexler was the best prospect I had so far, so why not him? I would need more information, of course. Financials and a formally drawn-up offer for me and the attorneys to go over, but that could come after a meeting between the two of us to hash out the details. "What's your schedule look like? Can we set up a time to discuss this further, face-to-face, when we've got some hard numbers at hand?"

"I'd like that," Bexler said, then suggested times from his calendar. "Unfortunately, I'm headed out of town today and won't be back until the end of next week. How about that Friday afternoon?"

"Sounds good." I pulled up my own calendar on my laptop and added in the time that we quickly agreed on. "See you then, Mr. Bexler."

After ending the call, I checked through my emails and saw a message from Jameson about an update. Rather than type out a response, I decided some exercise might do me good and headed downstairs myself to find out what had been uncovered. I found Jameson in his office, mulling over more stacks of paperwork and files.

I knocked, then entered and closed the door behind me. "Thought I'd come down myself."

"Right," Jameson said, gesturing toward the chair in front of his desk. "Have a seat, Mr. Shepperton. I did some digging into Carrie Bartlett, as you asked, and your hunches were right. She *did* get instructions from your brother, Devon." He shuffled through some files, then pulled one out to hand to me. "From what I can ascertain, there was a money laundering operation taking place through the Shepperton Foundation. Not of money from Shepperton, Inc., but funds from other sources. It looks like Devon tried to funnel the money into shell companies which he framed as charitable organizations. Following all of those money trails would be akin to going down a rabbit hole. It would take weeks, and it might just lead in circles. So, since time is of the essence in our situation, instead, I scrutinized the data I had immediate access to— Shepperton Foundation's incoming donations. Specifically, the ones that came in since your brother changed the foundation's policy on accepting outside donations."

"We didn't use to accept outside donations?" I asked.

"No. Since the foundation is an arm of Shepperton, Inc., the money has always come directly from the company's surplus revenue. Honestly, accepting outside donations is highly irregular for a company-affiliated charitable foundation, but your brother was able to convince the board that it was the right decision."

"So you think all of these donations are connected to the laundering scheme?"

Jameson shook his head. "I'm sure they're not. There's no better place to hide dirty money than in a pile of clean money. I'd imagine most of the donations are perfectly legitimate—but I was able to pull a list of the ones that Devon handled personally."

"Him handling the donation personally is a red flag?"

"A sizeable one," Jameson agreed. "He was generally happy to leave those details to the foundation staff. These are the names I found."

He passed a piece of paper over to me. On it were written the names of five local Dallas companies and one international company that I actually recognized: the Hayes Group. It was a private military group, offering logistical support, data collection—the works. SEAL Team Four had worked with a few of their mercs from time to time. Good guys on the whole, if a little rough. Considering the sizable contract they had with the government, I couldn't see the company using the foundation to launder money. For someone like Ian Hayes, the founder and CEO of the Hayes Group, the money in the Shepperton Foundation would seem like a drop in the bucket.

But there *were* other local companies that would need some looking into. I knew almost nothing about them. I scowled. I wanted to have this cleared up before I talked to Bexler, and a week and a half wasn't a lot of time. "Okay. So, we need to speak with all these CEOs, then?"

"Interestingly, sir, you don't," Jameson said. "My research showed there's a common thread connecting all of them. Dowd & Associates. That law firm represents all of these companies."

"Even the Hayes Group?"

Jameson nodded. "Their Texas branch, anyway."

"Damn." Why would an international company need a local law office to represent them? It might not be pertinent to what happened to Devon…but something about it itched at the back of my mind. There had been Hayes men in the RoW when we'd been there, though they hadn't been part of the extraction mission that had gone so badly. Still—

Focus, Drake. One thing at a time.

I shook my head and looked at the older accountant, my lips parting. Maybe we were finally getting somewhere on this after all. "Good. Let's make sure we have all of our documentation in order before we approach our legal counsel with this. I want them armed with everything to begin a full investigation into this mess." I stood and handed the file back to Jameson. "Thanks for all your hard work on this."

"Anytime, sir," the older accountant said. "I'll make up formal reports now."

EIGHTEEN
DRAKE

Back in my office, I made the call I'd been putting off for a long time.

Adrian Pierce was the SEAL who turned me into the CO that I'd become. He was maybe the smartest man I knew—sharp, focused, fiercely determined...and unendingly loyal. It was the last one that had come back to bite him in the end, when his loyalty made him blame himself for letting Kyle down and not keeping him safe during the mission.

It was also, according to Gabe Kelley, part of the reason why Adrian had chosen to become an FBI agent. He wasn't letting the mission go, and the resources he'd have as a Fed would let him get to the bottom of things—if there *was* any bottom to get to. I didn't want to think of what it might do to him if he got to the end of the road and found out that the mission going FUBAR was down to nothing more than shitty luck and bad timing—no grand conspiracy, just life not always going the way it should.

But whether being an FBI agent ended up bringing him peace and closure or not, the fact remained that he was an agent now…and that meant that he was someone I could turn to for help.

I opened my contacts and found the number that Gabe had passed my way: I pushed 'call,' and then sat back in my office chair while the call rang through.

Adrian answered on the second ring. "Agent Pierce."

"Adrian?" I said, hearing his voice brought back memories from being out on the battlefield with the guy. Somehow, I always felt reassured when I heard that voice. "It's Drake Shepperton."

"Drake?" Adrian sounded genuinely surprised. "Gabe passed my number to you?"

"You know that he did."

He chuckled. "You called from the States. Where the hell are you? Last I heard, the unit was overseas."

"They are, but I'm in Dallas, dealing with a death in the family."

"Oh." He sobered up. "Of course—I'm sorry. I heard about that in the news; I just didn't make the connection. What was he, a cousin or something?"

"Twin brother, actually."

"Yikes. My condolences."

"Thanks, I appreciate that." I sat forward and exhaled slowly. "Listen, I was hoping you could help me out with something."

"Sure. Anything for a teammate. Hang on." Adrian put his hand over the mouthpiece and said something to someone, then came back to me. "Sorry. Busy day here today. What can I do for you?"

"Well, my brother ran the family business, and since I'm the only Shepperton left, it's up to me to figure out what to do with it now. I've been acting as CEO since I got back, and I've come across some things in the company's accounts that appear…troubling." I scrubbed a hand over my face, then went on to tell Adrian about what I'd found and the possible money laundering taking place through the Shepperton Foundation. "I would've contacted you sooner, but things have been nuts lately."

"I get it, man." Adrian sighed. "And wow. That's a lot of suspicious activity you got there. Have you contacted the police?"

"Not about the laundering. I didn't want to start a stink until I knew for sure that there was something there. In the meantime, I was trying to deal with it myself."

"You and Kelley," Adrian said with a snort. "You two always have to do things on your own, don't you? Gotta be in control of the situation. I should've guessed that you were part of the most ruthless business family in Texas. Funny how you never mentioned that to us."

I hung my head. I didn't like secrets any more than I liked being compared to my rotten family, but Adrian did have a point. I *did* like being the one in control. "Look, I didn't mention it because I didn't want to be treated differently. I'm not like the rest of my family. All they ever cared about was getting ahead and getting as much money as they could. Whoever got in the way of that got kicked aside or trampled." My gut clenched when an image of Layla flashed into my head. She was the last victim of Devon's machinations, but thanks to the twins, she'd carry the reminders with her for the rest of her life. I so wished I could have been the one to make things better for her. I missed her so much my chest ached with it, but I'd told her the truth. Things couldn't work between us. Not if I wanted to keep her safe. "Anyway, I need this mess cleaned up before I can sell Shepperton Inc. and I'd like your help to do that. Are you in?"

"Well, I'd like to help, Drake. But money laundering falls under the jurisdiction of the Treasury Department. If you want, I can pass you over to—"

"No." The word came out harsher than I'd intended. "I want the fewest people involved in this as possible. At least until I know exactly who's involved and how deep the corruption goes. If you can't help me, I'll keep dealing with it myself."

Adrian exhaled slowly. "Officially, there's nothing I can do."

"What about unofficially? I think we both know that you're not above using the resources you have for side projects."

Adrian was quiet for a moment, and then a deep chuckle issued over the phone line. "Unofficially, I'll look into it when I can. What are those names again?"

I read them off, then set the reports aside. "If you can check the companies out and let me know what you find—any fines, indictments, rumors of wrongdoing—I'd appreciated it. There's one that may pique your interest. You remember the Hayes Group?"

"Yeah…rough rider mercs, right?"

"Yep. Why would a big, international conglomerate like that need to employ a Texas law office? They're not even based here."

"That is interesting, but I'm not sure what that it has to do with me."

"I remember when we were in the RoW that the Hayes Group had an outcrop there. It's probably nothing, but Gabe told me that you're spinning your wheels looking into that mission. Maybe Hayes knows."

"They weren't there that day, Drake." Adrian's voice was rough now. *Shit.* I hadn't meant to upset him.

"I didn't say they were, but maybe they got some intelligence that we didn't. It would give you a place to start, right?"

Adrian was quiet again, to the point that I thought he hung up on me. "It's an idea," he conceded. "Meanwhile, I have something that maybe *you* could help me with."

"You're helping me," I said, "it would be gauche not to offer a helping hand in return."

Adrian snorted. "Gauche," he scoffed. "You're such a tool. Why'd they put you in charge again?"

"Because I learned from the best," I said with so much sincerity that it made us both pause. I cleared my throat. "What do you need, Adrian?"

"Do you remember the package we were trying to extract during the mission?"

"An informant, right?" I asked. "He got shot down during the ambush, didn't he?"

"That's right. His name was Anton Koza."

"Okay, what about him?"

"Well, he said some really weird shit to me while he was bleeding out. At first, I thought it was just nonsense. It definitely didn't make sense, but then he told me, just before he died, that nothing is what it seems. That we were missing the big picture. That part was totally clear."

"So you're thinking that maybe the weird bullshit wasn't just the words of a hallucinating dying man?"

"Exactly. I tried looking him up to see what he was involved in, maybe see if I could piece together some of what he was saying, but he'd been scrubbed from the federal system."

Okay, admittedly, that was weird. I'd been pretty skeptical about Adrian's quest up to this point, but maybe he was on to something.

"Now I'm wondering if Koza was passing along a coded phrase or something."

I could see where he was going. "Coded phrases aren't exactly firewalls that I can de-encrypt. It's just words."

"But if you thought about it like a computer program, could you try and make some sense of it?"

Code breaking was a skill set that I dabbled in, though I couldn't claim to be a true master at it. "I can work on it. Run it through a few of my programs."

"Thanks, Drake. I'll send it to you. Do you have a secure email?" I gave it to him. "In the meantime, I'll work on your brother's money laundering. I'll be in touch when I know something."

"Yep." I thanked him and ended the call. Okay. One problem tackled…and another put on my plate. But that could wait. Right now, I needed to get with Layla about all this too. I'd put off seeing her as long as I could today, even though I could hear her bumping around in her office next door. Time to man up and get it over with.

I took a deep breath and stood, grabbing the reports from the desktop and heading for the door as an old SEAL motto rattled through my head. I'd heard it millions of times over the past few years, but it had never hit quite so close to home as it did now.

The Only Easy Day Was Yesterday.

And wasn't that the truth. Every day with Layla up until yesterday had been easy. Or at least eas*ier.* Then I'd gone and fallen in love with her. Despite my wishes and intentions to the contrary. And now things were awkward as ass between us because of me and my speech in the bedroom last night. Dammit.

I should've kept my hands to myself and my heart out of it, but where Layla was concerned that hadn't been an option. She'd stormed my defenses and broken through all my barriers. I halted on the threshold of my office, the muted sounds of Layla's voice as she spoke with someone on the phone in her office echoing into the hallway. My ribcage constricted, seizing the air in my lungs. If things were different, if *I* were different, maybe we'd have had a chance. As it was, once this was over, there'd be nothing left between us but goodbye.

A few weeks ago, that would have made me feel happy. Now, it made me feel anything but.

Layla

The knock on my office door made me glance up from the computer screen. "Yes?"

Drake poked his head around the door and my heart sank. My first instinct was to get up and walk over to him, throw my arms around him, and kiss him silly. Except things weren't like that between us anymore. He'd told me in no uncertain terms our affair was over, and the sooner I accepted that and moved on, the better.

I gave him what I hoped was my most professional smile. "What can I do for you, Mr. Shepperton?"

His expression tightened slightly at my use of the formal title, but he quickly covered it. He walked into my office and shut the door behind him, then handed me a sheet of paper. "I met with Jameson earlier and he gave me this."

"Huh." I scanned the page, noting that it listed five of the foundation's most generous donors. "You think all of these were involved in the operation?"

"Not sure yet, but from what Jameson told me, it seems likely." Drake slumped down in one of the chairs in front of my desk, the faint lines at the corners of his dark eyes and around his lips more pronounced today. There were dark circles beneath his eyes too. I wondered if he'd slept as badly as I had the night before but didn't dare ask. There was enough tension around us as it was. No sense adding more to the pile. He rubbed his jaw and stretched his long legs out in front of him. Even knowing he wanted nothing more to do with me sexually didn't stop the rush of lust searing through me at the sight of him in his perfectly tailored suit. Damn, but the man looked fine. I shook off the inappropriate thoughts and frowned down at the reports once more, determined to stay on track and out of the smutty pool where he was concerned.

When I didn't answer, Drake continued. "I also called in a friend to check out those companies marked in the report. He's an old SEAL teammate who now works for the FBI."

"FBI doesn't handle money laundering," I said, without thinking. At his pointed silence, I glanced up to find him watching me with a narrowed gaze.

"How do you know that?"

Crap. I hadn't told him about my parents' crimes, and now I wouldn't either. He *might* have had some right to learn about my past back when we were lovers, but we were nothing more than business colleagues at this point, so I tried to play it off as best I could. I shrugged. "I watch a lot of crime shows on TV."

"Hmm." He sounded decidedly unconvinced, but thankfully let it go. "Anyway, my friend Adrian said he'd do some checking into those companies anyway, then let me know if he turns up anything suspicious. He's also going to try and track down Carrie Bartlett and question her. See what she knows."

"Good." I set the reports aside and went back to typing on my computer. "Anything else?"

"Do you recognize any of those company names on the reports?"

"Of course." I said, clack-clacking away. "It's my business to know all of our donors."

"You didn't mention that the foundation had only recently started accepting outside donations."

"Well, yes," I said. "From what I understand, it started a few years ago. I've only been with the foundation for the past two years, so it predates me. I guess I forgot that it hadn't always been that way."

Drake continued to stare at me, his dark gaze unreadable. The quiet grew suffocating, and his stare burned a hole through me as I worked, and the moment stretched taut. Heat prickled my cheeks. *Please don't let him ask me how I'm doing. Please don't.* Because if he asked, I was feeling vulnerable enough right then that I just might tell him. Tell him I felt heartbroken and lonely and missed him so much I hurt with it. And that wouldn't do either of us any good.

Luckily, he didn't ask. Instead, he changed topics to something that surprised me completely. "I may have found a buyer for Shepperton, Inc."

I stopped short, my fingers freezing on the keyboard as I met his dark eyes. "Really? Who?"

"Man by the name of Baron Bexler. Big-time rancher. He was at the gala last night. Ever heard of him?" Drake asked, sitting back in his seat, his broad shoulders slumping a bit as he stared down at his hands in his lap.

"No. And pretty much everyone who's got money down here has some connection to ranching." I swiveled in my chair to face him. I'd known he'd been searching for a buyer but hadn't expected him to find one so quickly. One more task completed. One more nail in the coffin of our time together. "So, he sounds serious then?"

"Seems to be. I've set up another meeting with him to formally discuss things, since we first met when we were a few drinks in, which really wasn't conducive to talking business." He sat forward again, the expensive material of his suit stretching tight over his muscled arms, and my pulse stuttered once more. I swallowed hard and looked away fast. "Do me a favor?"

Anything. The word teetered on the tip of my tongue before I forced it away. If Drake had a good lead on a buyer for Shepperton, Inc. and we were narrowing down leads on his brother's illicit activities, then that meant that his responsibilities in the area were quickly wrapping up. Even more reason to stick with his new plan to put distance between us. Too bad my stupid heart had other ideas. I had come to care for him far too much, far too quickly, and that was bad. So bad. Because caring too much for people only led to pain and regret, in my experience. And I had more than enough regret in my life already. Besides, now I had more than myself to think about. I had my babies. My hand drifted down to rest atop my stomach as Drake stood and headed back toward the door.

He stopped part way, though, and turned back to me, a flash of hurt in his dark eyes before he covered it again. Drake opened his mouth to say something, then closed it again. A weird mix of apprehension and adrenaline buzzed inside me, waiting for him to speak. There was so much left unsaid between us, even after our talk in the bedroom; so much inside me I'd never say because having the words out there, saying out loud that I loved him, might break me beyond repair.

"Layla," he said at last, my name sounding like a cross between a blessing and a curse. His dark brows drew together, and his lips compressed into a thin line. "I don't regret what happened. With us."

The hardest thing I'd ever done was turn away from him again, but I did. Swiveled right back to face my computer, hoping the distance between us and the computer screen would hide the tears welling in my eyes. I didn't want to cry. Not now. But I couldn't seem to stop myself. "There is no 'us.' Not anymore, right? That's what you wanted. And now that I've thought about it, you're right. Things are complicated enough here without the added pressure of our affair. Let's stick with the plan, shall we?"

Drake stood there for several seconds. His internal battle was palpable to me because I was fighting the same battle inside. I was torn between the urge to run to him and hurl myself into his arms and never let him go—or to stay where I was and let him walk out of my life forever. In the end, we both remained on our separate sides of the divide.

"Yes. The plan," he said, turning away to open the door, his deep voice grumbling with finality. "We'll stick with the plan. Can you check into those companies in the report as well?"

Work. Yep. That was all we had now.

I nodded, not trusting my voice. The door closed behind him ,and I sat for a long while afterward, just staring at the wall and thinking I ought to feel a lot better about things than I did. Because right now, I felt like I'd just thrown away something precious and rare that might never return again.

Two days later, I sat in my office listening while Layla relayed the results of her research.

"Basically, all of these businesses were involved with a Shepperton, Inc. development project in Nevada," she said, her tone cool and professional, any sign of our previous passion gone. No flirting. No warmth. I should be relieved by that, but all I felt right now was a crappy hollowness gnawing inside me. She glanced up at me, her gaze icy. "That's not unusual, though, at least on the surface, since most of the donors to the foundation are involved with various projects in one way or another. It's the gateway for many of our partners into the foundation."

"Hmm." I frowned and took a deep breath. I caught a hint of Layla's sweet floral perfume on the air, but I did my best not to focus on it. Tried not to focus on how nice she looked in her black pantsuit either, or the paleness of her complexion this morning. Was she feeling okay? Eating okay? Since our conversation the other night, she'd kept to herself, forgoing meals with me in favor of eating alone in her room at the condo. We'd barely said more than two words to each other outside of the office, and dammit, I didn't like it one bit. Even though it had been my decision to break it off, she was still carrying my brother's twins and I still felt responsible for her well-being.

And I missed her too.

Not that I'd ever tell her that. The fact that she seemed able to put up walls between us so easily when I couldn't seem to keep my mind from drifting to her every second of the day didn't help either.

I needed to keep my head clear and my brain on task at the moment, what with this shitstorm Devon had left behind. I'd thought ending things with Layla would make concentrating easier to do, but the distance between us only seemed to bother me more. I'd slept like shit last night and food tasted like cardboard when she wasn't there to smile at me across the dinner table. Honestly, I felt more distracted now, without Layla, than I had before.

It made no sense. If I didn't know better, I'd think I was in love. Except that wasn't possible. I'd gone into this whole thing knowing it was temporary. I didn't do love anyway. And maybe if I told myself that enough times, the ache in my chest would subside.

"Anyway," Layla continued, drawing me out of my thoughts. "From my end, all of the donation activity from these companies looks normal. The only possible red flag would be the large amounts."

Shit.

I opened my mouth to answer, but the buzzing of the phone on my desk cut me off. Layla started to leave, but I held up a finger to stop her. Reluctantly, she slumped back down into her chair and fiddled with her reports while I answered the call without looking at the screen.

"Drake Shepperton."

"Hey, it's Adrian. I looked into those names you gave me, and I got a hit."

"Yeah?" I sat forward, a spark of interest shoving aside the heavy weight of regret inside me. Layla glanced up at me, her brows raised and her expression curious. I put the call on speaker phone and laid it on the desk. "Tell me. I've got an associate here with me who's helping me with the internal investigation."

"Right," Adrian said. "After we talked, I got those names over to a buddy I went through training with—he got placed in the White Collar Crimes unit. They work in conjunction with the Treasury Department on some of these cases. Turns out they've been monitoring four of the companies on the list you gave me."

Layla sat forward too, giving me a view down the front of her blouse. I swallowed hard and looked away. "Go on," I said, my voice rougher than normal.

"The thing that really stood out to the unit, though, was the name of the law firm you said connected all of them—Dowd and Associates. Turns out the guys in White Collar Crimes have had Felix Dowd under surveillance for the past six months on suspicion of fraud."

I scrubbed a hand over my face. Finally, the pieces were coming together. Determination to put an end to my brother's injustices burning in my gut, I nodded. "Good. What's our next step, then?"

"The unit wants to set up a video call with you to discuss your reports and gather more evidence," Adrian said. "What's your schedule look like for Friday?"

After pulling up my calendar and checking the day, I set up an appointment for Friday afternoon, then ended the call. Layla still sat across from me, oddly quiet now that the new information we'd been searching for was out there. I could feel the weight of her stare prickling on the side of my face until I finally glanced her way. Her frown had darkened, and shadows filled her brown eyes. I figured maybe she was upset because I'd dominated the conversation, so I said, "You can attend the meeting too on Friday, if you're available."

"I'll have to check my calendar," she said, standing. "What about the company's legal counsel?"

Damn. I'd forgotten about them. Before she left, I picked up my phone again and called the company attorneys to tell them about the FBI's findings and the Friday afternoon meeting. Once I hung up, I stood and walked around the desk to catch Layla before she opened the door.

"The attorney's advised that we suspend all donation activity to the Shepperton Foundation until after the meeting on Friday," I said, hiding my wince. That foundation was everything to Layla. Having it mired in scandal now because of my asshole brother had to be killing her. "I'm sorry."

"It's fine," she said, though her brisk tone and the fact she wouldn't meet my gaze clearly said it was not. "I should get back to my office and get started, then. I've got lots of phone calls to make."

She exited, leaving me behind to stare after her, my initial happiness at having my suspicions confirmed dulled by more regret. I couldn't help but regret hurting Layla more after what I'd already done. Maybe I could make some calls, find her a new foundation to run—a new career to replace the one I'd destroyed.

Damn you, Devon. Damn you to hell and back.

Restless and frustrated, I stalked back to my desk. The one thing I still couldn't figure out was why the hell my brother had done it. Devon wasn't a saint by any means, but he was also rich by any definition of the word. He didn't need the extra cash. Plus, money laundering took a lot of planning and effort, neither of which my brother had been too keen on in his life. Devon liked things with as few complications as possible. Devising this elaborate scheme seemed way outside his wheelhouse. Even with the help of Carrie Bartlett, it seemed beyond Devon. So, was there someone else helping him to funnel the funds through the company?

An image of Layla flashed into my mind again, but I quickly shoved it aside. No way. She'd been through enough where my brother was concerned. There wasn't a chance in hell she'd have helped him, even if they had been sleeping together. Besides, I'd seen her personnel file. Everything had checked out clean. She was the one who had come to me with the initial suspicions—I wouldn't even have looked into this if she hadn't brought it to my attention in the first place. Beyond question, she wasn't involved.

I wasn't the kind of guy who enjoyed questions in life. I was an answer man through and through. Perhaps that's what bothered me most of all about this whole fucking mess. The uncertainty. The not knowing. The uncomfortable realization that I didn't know who I could trust anymore.

Except Layla. You trust her completely.

It was true. I did. After what we'd been through together the past couple of weeks, there was no one I wanted on my side more. Even if I'd soon walk away and never see her again.

With a sigh, I plopped back down in my seat and reached for my phone once more. I needed to fill Jameson in on the call with Adrian and the meeting Friday, since I wanted the accountant there as well.

I returned to my office feeling even more discombobulated than I had before. It wasn't just the thing with Drake. It was the fact that all of this would be over way sooner than I'd imagined, based on that phone call I'd just heard.

And speaking of phone calls, I needed to start making some myself.

Hoping to distract my mind from the yawning cavern my future had become, I kept busy calling all of Shepperton, Inc.'s current donors—with the exception of the companies on the list Drake had given me—and informing them that all fundraising activities were on hold until further notice. When questioned about why, I told them that the foundation was reevaluating its future due to Devon's death. Not the truth, but not a complete lie either. All of this mess had started with his car accident.

No, that wasn't true.

The mess had started the minute Devon had made his choice to launder that money. Then, of course, I'd had my own moment of idiocy in sleeping with the guy. Not that the two were connected, but still.

Looking back now, I could see how foolish it had been. I sat back and rubbed a hand over my belly. Not that I regretted everything about our ill-advised union. Sleeping with him had given me the twins and I wouldn't trade them for anything. And the twins had eventually led me to meeting Drake Shepperton. Even though it was all over for us now, I didn't regret that either.

Honestly, the only thing I regretted here was the fact that the job I loved would soon vanish.

With a sigh, I picked up the phone again to make another call, only to hang up. It all felt so pointless now. Pointless and exhausting. Given that the FBI was now involved and Shepperton, Inc. was up for sale, it was unlikely the foundation would survive. Maybe I should just let it die a quick death and move on.

I reached over and tapped the keyboard on my computer, bringing up the file directory. One more click and my old resume appeared onscreen. Whatever the fate of the Shepperton Foundation, I needed to make sure I had a job that would ensure adequate finances for the months ahead. Twin pregnancies by nature were higher risk than single births and my OB/GYN had already talked to me about the possibility of bed rest as my due date grew closer. This early, I felt fine, but as the pregnancy progressed, I was at a higher risk for complications. If the worst-case scenario happened, I'd need to be prepared.

Always thrifty, I had saved a tidy nest egg that should cover the last trimester if I ended up not being able to work during that period, and six months of post-partum leave, but then I'd need to get another job if this one fell through, which seemed likely. Plus, I'd need health insurance for me and the twins. Hopefully I could negotiate my severance package from Shepperton, Inc. to include coverage for a year paid by the company. Drake owed me that, at least, and I didn't think he'd fight me on it.

Right. Never one to wallow in my troubles, I straightened and faced down my outdated resume. Knowing the foundation was in trouble, it wouldn't hurt to put out feelers now to see if anyone was hiring. If I could have something lined up to move over to right away, I could get my feet wet and start establishing myself before my pregnancy became a serious concern. Maybe I could even work through the last trimester, if my new employer was flexible about letting me work from home. Non-profits were my specialty, but at this point I wouldn't be picky. Basically anything that would pay the bills and offered a full benefits package was on the table. Never mind I might be overqualified. Post-graduate degrees didn't mean squat when you couldn't put food on the table.

My gut clenched and my shoulders tightened. I gave an ironic snort. Funny, but I'd spent so many years trying not to end up like my parents and here I was, one company closure away from being right back where I started. Desperate and alone. Just like my parents.

They'd turned to a life of crime to get what they needed.

I refused to do the same.

Old fears burned the back of my throat, but I swallowed hard and continued typing the new information on my work for the Shepperton Foundation into the resume template on my computer. Considering there could be huge fallout once Devon's illicit activities were made public, job hunting became a top priority. The last thing I needed with everything else going on was for my career prospects to get caught in the crossfire.

Without thinking, I placed a hand on my tummy again as I typed one-handed. I needed to look out for myself now. Myself and the twins. We'd be on our own soon enough and I needed to make sure I had a plan to keep us all safe and secure.

Drake

I was running. Literally and figuratively.

Anxious to burn off some excess energy and give myself time to clear my head, I'd left the office shortly after my phone call with Jameson about the FBI meeting on Friday and had headed down to the company gym in the basement. Lifting weights and kickboxing had done little to sweeten my sour mood, however, so I'd abandoned the indoors and headed across the parking lot to the outdoor track running through the local park instead.

The weather was nice enough, with sunshine and blue skies above, and soon I'd worked up a good sweat as I completed my eighth lap around the half-mile track. The steady pound of my heart matched the rhythm of my footfalls on the pavement and helped ground my mind. By the time I ran four more laps, my lungs burned and blood pounded in my ears, but the same old conflict tore me up inside.

Man, this whole thing had me torn and twisted like never before, and it wasn't just the stuff with Devon either. My yearning for Layla had become a physical ache inside me, urging me to do something stupid like rush back to her office and beg on my hands and knees for her to take me back.

Which was ridiculous. Her aloofness today had proven that she'd put me and our affair behind her, and I needed to do the same. The sooner the better. Now if only I could get my heart on board with that plan, I'd be all set.

I slowed to a walk, then stopped near the bench where I'd set my towel and water bottle. I'd just finished wiping off my face and draining half my water in one long gulp, when the crack of a bat hitting a ball echoed from somewhere nearby. I scrubbed away the sweat stinging my eyes with the towel, then moved back a few steps to peer around the fence toward a baseball diamond across the field from the track. I'd been so preoccupied earlier, I hadn't even noticed it was there. A guy was over there with his son, helping him practice his hits.

I stood there for a minute or so, watching them while I caught my breath, loneliness pinching my chest. When I'd been young, I'd have given anything to have my dad take me out to play ball like that. But my father had always been too busy working to spend time with his kids. Or at least, to spend time with me, doing any of the things that interested me. Our dad had plenty of time to spend with Devon, taking him to the office and showing him how things worked in the company. At first, he'd wanted to take me too, but business had never been my thing. Not then. Not now either.

Taking a deep breath, I turned away and walked back over to grab my towel, then head back to the office to shower and change. I still had a stack of paperwork to get through and spreadsheets to make for my meeting with Baron Bexler the following week. I barely made it two steps, though, before someone yelled my name.

"Drake? Is that you? Drake Shepperton?"

Halting, I turned back, frowning as the dad from the baseball diamond jogged toward me.

As the man neared, recognition dawned—and my crappy day got a little bit shittier.

Billy Martin. My old friend. The one whose dad had gotten hurt on the job at Shepperton, Inc., then screwed over by my father and the system. Perfect. I hadn't seen the guy in years and would have tried to avoid a reunion this time too, but fate obviously had other ideas.

With a sense of dread, I waited while the man and his little boy approached, feeling even worse about all the horrible things my family had done in the name of profit, if that were possible.

"Drake?" Billy said as he neared, his smiled widening. "It is you. I thought so. It's Billy. How you been, man?"

"Good. Thanks," I said, shaking his hand.

"Sorry to hear about your brother," Billy said, crouching next to the little boy from the ball diamond. He looked maybe six or seven. "This is my son, Hal."

I smiled down at the kid. He looked just like Billy had at that age, scruffy blond hair and freckles. "Hi, Hal."

"This is Drake. He and I used to be friends when we were your age."

The kid blinked up at me, then shrugged and pointed at the vending machine nearby. "Can I get a soda, dad?"

Billy straightened and pulled some money out of his wallet. "Here. But don't tell your mom, okay?"

"Okay." Hal ran off toward the vending machine, leaving us alone.

"So, you're back in town to deal with your brother's estate, huh?" Billy asked, squinting at me in the sunshine.

"Yep." I frowned down at my water bottle, waiting for the attack that didn't seem to be coming. The way we'd left things back in the day hadn't been good. Billy had been angry on his father's behalf and I couldn't blame him one bit. I wouldn't have blamed Billy for still being angry now—but strangely enough, it seemed that he wasn't. The anger that had simmered between us back then seemed to have dissipated over time. If there was a way I could go back and fix things, I would, but it was all water under the bridge now. Same as so many things these days. When Billy didn't say anything more, I hazarded a glance up at his old friend. "How are you these days?"

"Good. Good." Billy kept an eye on his son, who'd grabbed a bottle of grape soda from the machine and was cracking open the lid. "Working for the local auto plant. Coaching my son's little league team at night and on the weekends. Married twelve years now. Can't complain."

"That's great." I was happy for him. "I'm glad you're doing well."

"Me too," Billy said, and my breath caught in my chest. Uh-oh. Maybe *not* water under the bridge after all. But then my old friend clapped me on the shoulder. "Listen, I've been meaning to tell you for years, I'm sorry for how things got left between us. I was a pissed-off teenager who didn't know any better. I wanted to blame someone for what happened to my dad, and you were an easy scapegoat. I owe you an apology for that. I know you had nothing to do with it. There was nothing you could've done."

"Maybe not." I stared off into the distance and shook my head. "But it didn't make me feel any better about what happened, either. My dad and his company screwed over your family. No two ways about it. And there's nothing for you to apologize about. I should be the one telling you I'm sorry. Because I am." I took a deep breath. "That whole thing was why I left town. I couldn't stand to be around them anymore, knowing how they treated your dad. Made me sick. I wanted no part of them or their business. Would've stayed gone too, except with my parents gone and then Devon's accident, there was no one else to settle things here so…"

"So, the prodigal son returns home at last." Billy chuckled and hiked his chin toward the track. "Though still running, I see."

I snorted. "Yeah."

"Yeah." Another kid from the baseball diamond came over and he and Hal sat on the bench nearby while Billy and I talked.

"I'm selling Shepperton, Inc.," I said after downing another swig of water.

"Really?" Billy narrowed his gaze again. "Why?"

"Because I want no part of it. That life was never me. Never."

"Hmm." Billy crossed his arms and nudged a stone with the toe of his sneaker. "I suppose it is easier to hand things over than to put in the work to fix them and build them back up the right way."

I frowned. "What the hell is that supposed to mean?"

"Nothing." Billy looked away. "Just I remember when we were young, and you used to talk about all the things you'd do if you were in charge of the company. Things to make the community better. Things to help the workers. Can't do any of that if the place is closed, or if it belongs to someone else. We could really use a company with its priorities straight around here these days too."

"I can't." I exhaled slow and lowered my head. "Even if I wanted to stay, I've got other obligations. I'm up for another re-enlistment with my SEAL team, and there's no reason for me to turn that down now. Besides, I've got a potential buyer lined up for a meeting next week. I don't know anything about running a business. That was always Devon's thing. Not mine."

"Sure. I get that. We've all got stuff going on." Billy cocked his head. "Doesn't mean we need to abandon our old dreams though. Sometimes we just need to find a new path to happy."

"Hey, Dad, I gotta pee," Hal said, hopping down off the bench and walking back over to us.

"And that's my cue to leave," Billy said. He took his son's hand. "Well, it was great to see you again, man. If you have time before you leave town, give me a call. We can grab a beer or something." He rattled off his number and I typed it into my phone. "See you around."

"See you," I said, watching Billy and Hal walk away and feeling more confused than ever. As I gathered up my towel and headed back across the street toward the Shepperton offices, I couldn't seem to get my old friend's words out of my head.

Sometimes we just need to find a new path to happy.

I would love to regain the happiness I'd lost, but it all seemed impossible at the moment. I had too much going on, too much to deal with, too many wrongs to make right. There was no time to stop and think and plan what I wanted for the future. I had meetings and sales to make and a SEAL team who were waiting for me to re-up for four more years. Even if Adrian, Gabe, and Zach had jumped ship, the others needed me. Maybe after that, I could take a break, reassess, regroup. For now, though, my needs needed to take a back seat to my obligations to the company and the workers and Layla and the twins. Once those were settled, then I'd be on the first plane out of town and back to my old life again. Because that's what I wanted.

Isn't it?

TWENTY-ONE

DRAKE

By the time I got back to the office, it was well after five. I finished up some paperwork at my desk, then shut down for the night before heading next door to see if Layla was ready to leave. Even though her tires had been replaced, we were still riding together to and from work despite the issues between us. Whatever our relationship might be, I was still committed to keeping her as safe as possible, and that meant making sure she wasn't vulnerable to another attack.

She was just ending a call when I peeked inside her open doorway and she held up a finger for me to wait. "Yes, Ms. Adams. Thank you for your understanding. You can still make a donation directly to that charity by contacting the website I gave you. Thank you so much."

After she hung up, Layla sat back and yawned, looking about as tired as I felt. For a moment, I nearly walked over to massage her tense shoulders, maybe bend down and nuzzle her neck. Kiss away those slight frown lines at the corners of her mouth. Then I remembered things weren't like that between us anymore, by my own decision, and I dug my heels into the carpet to lock myself in place. It had been a long couple of days for both of us. I leaned a shoulder against the doorframe and glanced down the hall. The rest of the place was quiet since the staff had cleared out a while ago.

"You ready to go?" I asked.

"Yes. Sorry." She stood, her polite, professional mask quickly replacing the fatigue on her face. She was shutting me out again and it was just as well. Neither of us could afford to be vulnerable at this point. She logged off her computer and gathered her things, then joined me at the door, carefully avoiding my gaze. "Ready when you are."

"Great." The word sounded less than enthusiastic, but damn. I was doing my best here. To try and alleviate a bit of the awkward silence between us, I stuck to what I hoped were safer subjects. "How are the donors taking the news?"

Layla shrugged and stared straight ahead at the metal doors of the elevator as we descended toward the first floor. Her flat stare tugged at my heart, and I longed to see her sunny smile and fiery spirit again, no matter how dangerous they might be to my future plans. "About as well as can be expected," she said, her tone crisp. "The majority of people involved with the Shepperton Foundation are honest individuals who are truly devoted to making positive changes in the world. It's really horrible that a few bad actors ruined it all for everyone. My real concern, though, is for those who needed the grant money from our organization. I just hope other foundations will step in to fill the gap we've left behind."

"I'm sure they will," I said, holding the elevator open for her to exit first once we reached the lobby. "I can make a couple of phone calls as well tomorrow to see if I can urge some support, too."

"Thank you. That would be helpful." We walked out into the warm late spring evening and headed for my vehicle. There were only a couple of cars in the lot now, though it had been packed this morning when we'd arrived. I'd had to park at the end of the row, near a copse of bushes that lined the side of the building. I hit the button on my key fob and the headlights on the SUV flickered on and off. Layla avoided my gaze as we walked side by side, our arms occasionally brushing, sending sparks of awareness through my system despite my vows to steer clear of the connection still sizzling between us.

"Why is your hair damp?" Layla asked, after a glance in my direction.

"What?" The swift one-eighty in subjects knocked me off course for a second. "Oh." I reached up and ran a hand through my hair. "I went for a run earlier, then had a shower in the locker room."

"Oh." Now it was her turn to frown. "I didn't know you jogged."

"I don't. Not usually." I stopped near the front of the SUV. "I mean, I do when I'm away on missions, but not when I'm home on leave. I just needed to get out and clear my head, you know?"

Her eyes held mine for a moment before darting away again. "Yeah, I know."

The breeze stirred around us, rustling the leaves on the bushes nearby. Her sweet scent surrounded me, drawing me forward like a magnet and before I could think better of it, I took a step toward her, my focus solely on Layla at that moment. "Listen, I know what I said the other night, but..."

"Please." She held up a hand to stop me, her gaze lowered. "Let's not do this here, okay?"

"Okay, but—" I inched closer, vaguely aware of the rustling nearby getting louder even though the wind had died down, but the urgency inside was too strong to ignore. "Layla, I think maybe I was wrong."

That got her attention at last. Her brown eyes flew to meet mine, then widened with a combination of shock and fear. "Drake! Look out!"

Everything happened so fast, I had zero time to react. There was a sharp sudden pain on the back of my head, and my knees gave way. Next thing I knew, I was on the ground, the asphalt beneath my cheek biting into my skin and a warm stickiness slowly dripping down my face from a spot near my temple. My brain felt sluggish, and my thoughts were fuzzy. My body didn't want to cooperate with the voice bellowing in my head for me to get up. Get up and protect Layla.

She was screaming. I tried to lift my arms, tried to reach out to her, but my muscles refused to move. Darkness crept in from the corners of my vision, but I fought hard to stay awake even though my eyelids felt leaden.

Words. People were talking, but what were they saying? What was happening?

Danger! Danger!

For a second, reality shifted, and I was back on the battlefield, bombs and bullets exploding all around me, adrenaline and anxiety making the blood rush through my head. I'd been hit, wounded. That's why I was on the ground. Had I been shot? No. The only pain I had was in my head. They'd struck me on the head.

Must help my team. Must get up. Must save…

My consciousness wavered again, and I found myself back on the rough pavement. Over the pounding of my pulse, I strained to make sense of the conversations around me. It was all a blur until one sound stood out above the others, one I recognized all too well. The *snick* of a gun being cocked.

"No!" Layla said, her clear voice cutting through the growing fog in my head. "Don't shoot him. You can't. We…we need him."

My heart tripped.

What the—

No. I refused to believe she was involved in this mess. I'd had her checked out. I'd trusted her.

"There is no 'we', lady," a gruffer male voice said.

Layla's sharp laugh grated on my already overtaxed nervous system. I tried to lift my head, to see who our attackers were, but it felt like it weighed a ton. I managed to grunt, though, and earned a kick to the gut for my trouble.

Bastards.

"Are you so sure about that?" Layla continued, sounding different than I'd ever heard her. Harder. More brittle. She chuckled again, the sound unpleasant. "Listen, I'm glad you finally showed up again."

Again? I struggled to remember, and my whirling thoughts finally settled on the attack outside the condo, and the one outside the event. It must be the same men. The same men sent by Dowd and Associates. My heart rate kicked up another notch. Why had she said it like that? Was she trying to give me clues? Or was I fooling myself?

"Now I can drop the act," she said. "Thank God. Talk about a shitty job, pretending to like this asshole. I thought his brother was bad, but Drake's ten times worse. Selfish, lazy, and stupid. A dipshit trifecta."

This got a snort from our attackers and the tension in the air eased. The thug nearest me in my limited line of sight shuffled his feet and the sound of a gun being holstered followed.

"So, about the money." The toe of Layla's high-heeled pump tapped against the ground. "Don't look so surprised, guys. I know that's what you want and that's why you need me. You didn't mean to kill Devon, did you? I'm guessing you just wanted to scare him—but he was too dumb to wear a seatbelt, so when he crashed, the airbag snapped his neck. That's one problem solved because he can't make trouble for you anymore, but then you panicked when you realized you had no way to get the money without him. Don't worry—I can access all those accounts and withdraw the funds. I'm happy to cooperate too, for a price."

"Lady, we ain't about to negotiate here. We've got orders from our boss to take this guy out and bring you back with us."

"Yeah, but what if you don't kill him after all?" The thugs started to protest, but Layla stopped them. "No. Hear me out. I know this man has been a thorn in your side. Believe me, he's been a problem for me, too. I just wanted a second to myself so I could try to reach out, come to some kind of accord with your boss, but I couldn't shake the bastard, no matter how hard I tried. But killing him—it's not the answer. Murder is messy. And two brothers from the same family dying so close together would draw a huge amount of publicity—and law enforcement scrutiny—that I'm sure your boss would like to avoid. So, why not keep this one alive and use him as patsy?"

"Huh?" one of the men said.

"Keep Drake Shepperton alive—and pin all the crimes on him. Makes perfect sense. That way, we can take not only your boss's money back, but empty the foundation accounts completely." Her toe stopped tapping and she moved closer to the man standing on my left. "It's perfect and gives you all a tidy little profit on the side. Your boss doesn't have to know. What do you say?"

"I don't know," another man said, his voice deeper than the others. "Why should we trust you?"

"Because my real name is Layla Turner, and my parents were Ruben and Madelyn Turner. Ring a bell?"

I squeezed my eyes shut, trying to place those names. They sounded familiar but I couldn't get my mind to work properly at the moment. Luckily, the goon squad above me supplied the answer.

"Holy shit!" the first thug said. "You're the Turners' daughter?"

"None other."

"Damn," thug two responded. "I remember when they got convicted. They were fucking legends in the trade. Conned more people out of their life savings than everyone else on the West Coast combined."

"Yep. And they taught me everything they knew before being locked away," Layla said, her words a bit too bright and full of hollow pride to my ears. I'd known she'd been hiding something from me and now there it was. Fuck. Anger and betrayal welled up inside me and shook my steely conviction that Layla was on my side. If she'd lied to me about this, why not about the money too?

As if confirming my suspicions, she said, "I've been fooling him for weeks. Idiot doesn't know the first thing about laundering money or accounting. He doesn't have a clue what he's looking for, and he's so worried about making the company look bad that he's been afraid to ask anyone to do any digging for him. That made it so easy to misdirect his investigation. Like stealing candy from a baby. But it makes it all the easier to blame all this on him. He'll protest his innocence, of course, but who'll believe him? His family's cunning ways will bite him in the ass." Her tone turned pleading again. "C'mon, guys. Seriously. Don't turn down this opportunity. I can clear out the money tonight since everyone's gone, then manipulate the records to make it look like Drake was behind it all. You can even take me with you when you leave, as collateral for your boss to make sure I don't double-cross you. Maybe the cops will pin that on Shepperton too, blame him for my disappearance and send him to jail not only for embezzling the money but for kidnapping and murder too!" She laughed again and I winced, the shrill sound like nails on a chalkboard. "Hilarious, right?"

The thugs chuckled along with her, before the gruff one said, "You're a cold-blooded bitch, aren't you, lady?"

"Like parents, like daughter." Layla shuffled her feet. "Takes a pretty ruthless person to rob senior citizens of their retirement funds, yeah? Or how about when my mom and dad ran that con in Vegas? They were headlining at the Golden Nugget at the time, doing their magic show, and fleecing the vaults at the same time. Man, those were good times. No one knew how to pull a bait and switch like the Turners."

"Oh, yeah! I remember hearing about that one," thug two said. "Wished I could've gotten a piece of that action back then, but I was just a rookie."

"Then it's your chance at the big time now, buddy," Layla replied, manipulating the man to play right into her hands. She was good, I had to admit, even when she was bad. "What do you say? With a score this huge, you can both retire and do whatever the hell you want. No more bosses telling you what to do ever again." She went on from there, talking about how she'd move the money, what tricks she'd use to make it look like I was the one responsible. The men seemed enraptured by her and her plan.

I drifted in and out of consciousness as the thugs murmured in low voices to each other, discussing their options, until finally one of them reached down and yanked me off the ground by one arm. Pain sliced like a scalpel though my injured head, making me groan in agony and nearly pass out completely.

"Fine, lady," the first thug said. "We're in. What do we need to do, besides dump this guy somewhere no one will find him for a while?"

"I need to go back up to my office and use the computer there. You can watch me, if you still don't trust me."

"We don't," the thugs said in unison. "We're coming with you."

"Then just leave him in the backseat of his SUV here. He'll wake up in the morning with no idea what happened and a whole world of consequences to face."

"Right." The thugs opened the back door of the vehicle and tumbled me inside, my body ending up half on the seat and half on the floor, my face up toward the ceiling. They started to shut me inside, but Layla stopped them.

"Wait," she said, her voice sly and suggestive. "I want one last kiss." With a laugh, the thugs stepped back. I could sense Layla moving closer. Her warmth and scent surrounded me as she leaned over me. I vaguely registered her slipping something into the pocket of my suit jacket, but I was too muddled to do anything but lie there as she kissed my lips, her own cold against my skin. Then she was gone, and back outside the car again. Just before the door closed on me, I heard her say. "Good. Let's get to work then."

The slamming of the door was followed by muffled footsteps as the trio walked away, leaving me behind in the darkening car. Just before the throbbing in my head pulled me under for one final time into blessed sleep, I tried to reach for my pocket, but then the world went black, and my arm flopped uselessly at my side.

TWENTY-TWO

LAYLA

Back in my office, I did my best to concentrate on my computer screen and not the two bulky men leaning into my personal space near each shoulder. Or the fact that the man I loved was currently lying injured in the back of a car downstairs and there was nothing I could do about it.

I hadn't planned on using my parents' identity to save myself and Drake, but when the men had pulled that gun on him, I'd panicked and said the first thing that came to my mind that might make them stop. Now, I prayed I'd laid enough clues out there for Drake that he'd be able to figure out what I was really up to and end all this before it was too late. I didn't know how much he'd remember of what I'd said—honestly, I didn't know how much he'd even been conscious to hear—but I'd also had the presence of mind to record the whole incident in the parking lot on my phone before slipping the thing into Drake's pocket when I'd kissed him. It would be there waiting for him when he woke up.

If he woke up.

Man, there'd been blood. *So. Much. Blood.*

Head wounds bled profusely. I knew that, rationally. But they'd hit him so hard with the butt of that gun. Every time I closed my eyes, all I could see was Drake's face at the moment of impact. The surprise and sudden pain in his dark eyes, the way his body had slumped to the ground, lifeless at my feet. My stomach cramped and bile burned hot at the back of my throat, but I swallowed it down hard.

The worst thing I could do in the middle of a con was lose my shit. I needed to keep it together or both Drake and I would be dead before this was over.

My fingers shook slightly on the keyboard, bumping the wrong keys, but I corrected my mistake onscreen and kept going. Hopefully, Jameson down in accounting would be able to follow the tiny digital breadcrumbs I was leaving to track the funds I was currently rerouting out of the foundation's accounts into an offshore bank owned by one Felix Dowd. Between that and the phone, I hoped Drake would know that I'd never actually been involved in the money laundering. Of course, he'd also know that I came from a family of cons. After lying to him about my true identity for months, I didn't expect him to forgive me. But maybe, at least, the things I'd done would give him the truth at last and help absolve him of the crimes I was framing him for.

"Hurry up, lady," the larger of the two thugs said. He looked maybe forty and had a face resembling a bulldog. He also seemed to be the smarter of the two—which wasn't saying much—and was therefore the leader. He kept glancing back at my office door where the second thug was now standing to keep an eye out on the hallway. The staff was gone, but the cleaning crew would be arriving soon for the night. "We need to get out of here."

"I'm almost done," I said, the clack of my typing the only other sound in the room. My heart ached with each line I entered, wishing things between me and Drake hadn't had to end this way, wishing my life had turned out differently. Lord knew I'd tried. Tried to escape my past and my parents' legacy, but here I was, right back where I'd started. I entered the last set of commands, then hit send before logging out of the system entirely and shutting my laptop. "Done."

"Good." The second thug took my arm and all but dragged me toward the door. He was shorter and stockier. Also, his nose was black and blue, and he was breathing through his mouth, confirming that these two guys were most likely the same ones who'd attacked me and Drake in the parking lot a while back. "Let's go."

As we returned to the lobby and headed back outside to the thugs' vehicle, I couldn't help taking one final glance at Drake's SUV, still parked where he'd left it, no sign of life inside. I said a silent goodbye, knowing that this was truly the end for us. Even if he believed in my innocence, there was no way he'd ever want me back after this. I blinked back the sting of tears, then closed off my heart, the same way I'd learned to do as a kid. Cons and emotions didn't go together. I was on my own now. I had to make it through this, whatever it took. Not just for myself, but for my unborn twins as well. My parents might have failed me growing up, but I was determined to make a better future for my babies, no matter what it took.

I woke the next morning with a hell of a headache and an odd crick in my neck. I squinted into the sunshine trying to blind me and wondered where my curtains had gone. It took me a moment to realize there were no curtains because I wasn't at home. I was in the backseat of my car. I lay there a moment, my brain racing to grasp how I'd gotten there and why, but it was all a bit of a muddled mess at the present. The harder I attempted to force the memories the more nauseous I became, until I finally shut my eyes again and swallowed hard against the burning in my throat.

Eventually my stomach settled enough that I propped up on one elbow, allowing time for the dizziness to subside before sitting up all the way. Slowly, I reached back to feel the egg-sized lump on the side of my head, and a few of the pieces fell into place.

We'd been walking out to my car after work. Layla had been cold and distant, as usual these days. It had been late, and the lot was empty. I'd been about to tell her something and then…

Shit. My temples throbbed as if in sympathy.

Someone had bashed me on the head good. I winced, the movement in my cheek causing the dried blood there to pull against my skin. Honestly, given how long I was out, I probably had a fucking concussion. Ugh. Okay. So, I'd been knocked out and…

Layla!

My pulse tripped and I turned fast to survey the inside of the vehicle. Too fast. My stomach protested and this time I couldn't stem the tide of nausea roiling in my stomach. I barely got the door open before I retched on the pavement. Luckily, it was still early, and the lot was still deserted. Once I emptied my stomach, I wiped my mouth with tissues from the car, then leaned back against the side of the vehicle. God. What a fucking disaster. With all my SEAL training and experience, I should have suspected something was up, should have realized someone was lying in wait for us, but dammit. I'd been distracted lately. I lowered my head and took a deep breath, willing the shakiness in my hands to stop.

I needed to figure out who it was who'd attacked me, then find Layla.

Thoughts of her made my chest ache and my heart hurt. It also caused torrent of memory fragments to slice into my mind, none of them whole enough to make sense. Pieces of conversation—her saying that being with me was all an act, her agreeing to help the thugs. But why? Why would she do that?

Groaning, I rested my sore head back against the side of the SUV and closed my eyes again, concentrating on the scattered words stuck in my brain to make sense of them. Parents. She mentioned something about her parents. The Turners. Yeah, that was it. Her real last name was Turner.

I blinked my eyes open, my gut dropping to my toes. Oh shit. That made so much sense now. From the beginning I'd sensed she was holding a part of herself back from me, and now I knew why. The Turners' case had made national headlines back when they'd been convicted. They'd been ruthless thieves and had stolen from the most vulnerable. They'd made my own Shepperton clan look like a bunch of saints, and that was saying something. Thinking back on it, I thought I remembered something about their own daughter being the star witness against them. No wonder she'd wanted to distance herself from that past and bury it deep.

But more than anyone, I understood what it was like to try and escape your past and your family's legacy. Hell, that was exactly what I'd been doing when I'd joined the SEALs. I'd been upfront with Layla about it the whole time, and yet she'd still not trusted me enough to tell me the truth. That hurt worse than the lump on my head.

Cursing, I pushed off the vehicle and breathed in deep. Checking my watch, I saw it was going on seven a.m. Wherever Layla and the men who'd hit me were, they had a good twelve hour start on me. Best get back to the condo and get cleaned up before calling Adrian about all this. Common sense said I should probably see a doctor too, but there wasn't time for that now. I'd walk it off and get back to work, like the true soldier I was.

I started back around the car, then stopped again as something heavy in my suit jacket pocket flapped against my thigh. I kept my phone in an interior pocket, so it wasn't that. Frowning, I reached into it and pulled out Layla's phone. Another memory flashed in my head. Her leaning into the backseat to kiss me goodbye. The smell of her perfume filled my nose once more and I braced my free hand on the SUV to keep from stumbling. Why would she leave me her phone?

After climbing in behind the wheel, I started the engine, then clicked on her phone to see that the last app used had been a recording one. The latest recording was still up on the screen. Chest tight, I pushed the play button and heard the conversation between Layla and the thugs from the night before. Clever girl. She must've recorded the whole thing for me, then slipped the device in my pocket as a record. I still wasn't sure what to believe about her lying to me about her identity, but the fact that she'd given me this evidence had to mean something.

I listened to her words, picking out the clues she'd dropped without letting the thugs know what she was doing. Telling me exactly how she planned to move the money out of the foundation's accounts, where she planned to send it, what she'd input into the computer to make it look like I was responsible.

Damn. Pride swelled inside me, along with a sense of foreboding. I needed to get home and get in contact with Adrian, because shit was going to hit the fan and soon. I clicked off the phone and tucked it safely back in my pocket. The taped conversations should be more than enough to put the thugs and whoever hired them behind bars for a good long time, once I got it into the hands of law enforcement. First, though, I needed to get home and get cleaned up. I started to reach for my keys, but no. Driving was not in my best interest at the moment. I used the app to order an Uber instead.

Afterward, I blinked hard and rested against the rear of my SUV to allow the cool early morning breeze to keep me alert and focused while I waited. Adrian. I needed to let Adrian know what had happened. Hitting the redial button for my friend, I waited and waited, but he didn't pick up. Leaving a message wasn't ideal under the current circumstances, but it was better than nothing. I relayed the facts as best I could remember, then hung up just as my ride pulled up in an empty spot nearby. Thankfully the guy didn't ask too many questions, just gave me a few odd looks in the rearview mirror before we headed toward my condo. The traffic was light between the office and home, and I arrived within ten minutes. Layla was nowhere to be found, of course, but the fact that all of her stuff was still there in the guest room gave me hope she hadn't left town for good. Now, if I could just find her and make sure she was safe, I'd be all set. I checked my phone screen, but still no call from Adrian. I tried his number again, but still no answer.

Please let her be okay. Please let this all work out. Please…

After a quick shower and change of clothes, I felt almost human again. I popped a few aspirin and grabbed a bag of frozen peas from the freezer to hold on my sore head, then plopped down on the sofa in the living room and tried Adrian's number one more time. This time, he answered.

"Drake," Adrian said once he answered. "I just finished listening to your voicemail. Jesus, you never do anything the easy way, do you?"

"Easy is boring," I said, snorting, then wincing when it hurt my temple. "Listen, we need to find her. I don't believe she was in on the money laundering. Layla loves that foundation and she wanted to atone for the awful things her parents did. She'd never betray the charity like that."

"Okay. Well, I'd say our best is to stick with Dowd and Associates, since they're our top suspect in all this. I'd lay money that Felix Dowd is behind this at the end of the day." Adrian went silent for a minute, then got back on the line. "I've just texted my buddy with the connections in the Treasury Department. They're going to tap into the banking system to monitor transfers to and from the Shepperton Foundation accounts this morning. If your girl's clues pan out, then we should be able to track it all from here and trace them directly to Dowd. Then the local guys can pick him and his associates up for questioning."

I tossed the bag of peas aside and raked a hand through my hair. I hated waiting around, but there wasn't much choice. "Let me know when you have something, please."

"Will do," Adrian said. "Should probably get that head of yours looked at too. Maybe they knocked some sense into you at last."

"Funny. Not." I chuckled, then ended the call. Out of patience and restless, I spent the next couple of hours pacing the condo, making myself breakfast, then monitoring the local news for any signs of the cops picking up suspicious vehicles or Layla's abduction. Nothing.

God, why hadn't I told Layla earlier how I was feeling? Now, I might never get the chance to say what I needed to say to her, to tell her that I didn't care about who her parents were or the horrible things they'd done. She wasn't her family any more than I was mine. All that mattered now was us, together.

If she'd have me back. If we survived this.

Fuck.

She had to be terrified, out there alone with those men, playing a part to throw them off course, all to protect me when I should have protected her. My inner SEAL instincts railed against the failure.

No. I wouldn't fail here because I *couldn't* fail here. I would figure this out, with help from Adrian and the FBI and Treasury Department. I'd bring down Dowd and clean up the mess my brother had left behind. Then perhaps Layla and I could start fresh, make a new future for ourselves and the twins.

When I'd come home a few weeks ago, I had been so sure of what my plans were—sell the company, then re-up for another stint with SEAL Team Four. But now, nothing seemed sure. I'd never considered myself a businessman, but maybe I could run the company. My conversation with Billy the previous day had reminded me that once upon a time, I had dreamed about changing the world, or at least my little corner of it. Had dreamed about making Shepperton, Inc. a company to be proud of rather than despised. About making life better for our employees and empowering them to help others and better the community, too.

As I made yet another lap around the condo, the idea took root, blossomed. I started to see myself settling here in Dallas, maybe buying a house, starting a family—with Layla. It would be tough saying goodbye to my team, but now I felt ready to move on and start a new future.

But first, we had to end this fiasco.

After what seemed like a small eternity, but couldn't have been more than two hours, my cell phone buzzed. I answered on the first ring without checking the caller ID. "What's happening?"

"Anxious much?" Adrian laughed then sobered. "Don't worry. We'll get them. Promise. The transactions have started, just like your girl said on the recording."

My girl. Damn, that has a nice ring to it.

"And?" I said, my heart pinching with a fresh wave of yearning for Layla. "Can you trace them?"

"Yep. We're tracking them now." The sound of Adrian typing echoed over the phone line. "Looks like the signals are coming from a house over in University Park."

"Wait a sec, how do you know that? Aren't you in DC?" I asked.

Adrian chuckled. "Why do you think I was out of contact for a few hours? When I realized this was going down, I flew in to help. What, did you think I'd leave you to handle this on your own, brother?"

A rush of gratitude pulsed through me so hard that I couldn't speak for a minute. Of course I knew Adrian would come through for me when I needed him. Of *course* I knew that. Him being an FBI agent didn't change a damn thing about who he was. Just like I wouldn't have to give up who *I* was if I left the SEALs and became the permanent CEO. I'd still be there for my team—my brothers—whenever they needed me. I'd just be doing it from a home base now. That was something I'd never really had before. My parents' house hadn't really felt like home. But the one I wanted to build with Layla would. I was sure of that.

"Earth to Shep—you reading me, man?" Adrian said, intruding on my thoughts. "The guys from local Treasury department are putting a team together now to raid the place. You in?"

Like he even needed to ask. "Hell yes, I'm in. Just tell me where and when."

TWENTY-FOUR

LAYLA

I hadn't slept at all the night before, despite the opulence of my surroundings.

After I'd preauthorized the transfers through my computer at Shepperton, Inc.—something that could only be done on the company's network and something that the transfers wouldn't process without—the two thugs had brought me to this mansion set back in the woods on the outskirts of Dallas to complete the funneling of the money into their boss's account.

At least I didn't have to wait any longer to find out who was behind the whole money laundering scheme. Felix Dowd.

To look at him, he wasn't exactly what you'd call a classic villain. He was in his sixties, with a smallish stature and an unassuming face. I'd met him several times over the years at different charity fundraisers and hadn't thought twice about him. Which, looking back, was probably what made him such a genius crook. I'd learned early on from my parents that the best way to hide something was in plain sight. And Felix Dowd had obviously turned that wisdom into an art form.

He was sitting across from me in the massive chef's style kitchen at a granite island that could have seated six people and then some. The guy was reading the *Financial Times* and sipping a steaming mug of herbal tea, his blue eyes narrowed behind his wire-rimmed glasses.

"Would you like a piece of toast, my dear?" Dowd asked me without looking up. "Wouldn't want you going hungry in your condition."

The mention of the twins had me placing a protective hand over my abdomen. I wasn't showing too much at this point, but Dowd had had people watching me, obviously. My doctor's appointments must have given away my pregnancy. "No, thank you."

"Hmm." He turned pages in his paper and sipped more tea. "I hope the boys treated you well last night."

"The boys?" I tried to keep the snark from my tone and failed miserably. "You mean your thugs?"

"*Thugs* is such a base term." Dowd gave a dismissive wave, the silk sleeve of his expensive robe flapping gently. "How about guards?" He looked up at me at last, his icy gaze making me shiver. "Yes, I think I prefer bodyguards. Your thoughts, my dear?"

"My thoughts are that I'd like to get the hell out of here." I stopped short of telling him that I was not his dear and that his overly friendly tone made my skin crawl. "I've done what you asked."

"But the money is still in transit." Dowd set his paper aside at last and clasped his hands atop the cool granite countertop. "Until it clears my offshore accounts, you're not going anywhere." His eyes flicked down to my stomach again. "I assume Devon Shepperton is the father?"

I compressed my lips instead of responding, then countered with a question of my own. "Why are you doing this?"

Dowd blinked at me a moment as if confused. "Doing what?"

"Stealing money from charities that need it." I looked around at the extravagant house, the hand-painted tile floors, the high ceilings, the priceless artwork scattered everywhere. "You clearly don't need more cash."

"And that's where you're mistaken." He sat back and crossed his arms. As far as I could tell, we were the only two people in the house, though I didn't doubt there were numerous guards stationed outside for protection. Besides the two goons he'd sent after me and Drake last night, I'd seen several others patrolling the perimeter of the property out the window of my bedroom earlier. "One can never have too much money."

I snorted and shook my head. That sentiment was one I'd heard over and over from my parents while I was growing up. When they'd first started stealing and cheating people, it was because they'd needed the money to survive. But as their cons got bigger and more successful, their need had quickly transformed into greed. By the end, the funds they were taking from those elderly clients weren't even necessary. My parents had just done it because they could.

"Wrong," I said, biting the word out with a good portion of spite.

"And you're too idealistic, Miss Turner," Dowd said, using the last name I never wanted to hear again. "Would have expected better from you, knowing your esteemed lineage."

Exhausted and afraid, I couldn't restrain my emotions any longer. I all but growled, "Esteemed? Are you fucking kidding me? My parents were liars and cheats and frauds. There's nothing noble about that."

He tsked. "My dear. So ungrateful. Your parents were artists. They took what was basically a Ponzi scheme then added on the flair of a magical act and *voilà*. Perfection. The fact that you can't see the genius in what they did is your shortcoming, not theirs." He waved his hand again, as if my morals were nothing more than a bothersome fly to be shooed away. "You should embrace your past, use your talents as God intended and join me."

"Join you?" My bark of laughter was decidedly snide. "What are you? Some washed-up wannabe Bond villain? You're a petty thief, Mr. Dowd. That's all. A common criminal. And as soon as Drake Shepperton figures out what you're up to, he'll catch your ass and put you in prison for the rest of your miserable life." I shrugged. "Maybe you can bunk with my parents. I'm sure they could use a friend or two right now."

Straightening, Felix Dowd smoothed a hand down the front of his garish, embroidered silk robe and glared at me. "There is nothing common about me, Miss Turner. Nothing. And as far as Drake Shepperton goes, you saw to it yourself that he won't be coming after me. He'll be too busy clearing his own name." A small smile curved his thin lips, unpleasant and cruel. "Besides, you should be careful about throwing stones from your glass house. You were happy enough to climb into bed with Devon Shepperton, who was dirty as hell. The whole Shepperton family had no qualms about bending the rules to get what they wanted. Devon was exactly what you accused me of being. A thief and a criminal. He just happened to handle his business in the public eye. See what I mean about money? Get enough of it and people let you do whatever you want." One corner of his lips pulled up into a smirk. "Or *who*ever you want. You must be quite…persuasive to have seduced not just one Shepperton twin, but two. Nice work, Miss Turner."

Hackles up, I clenched my fists at my sides to keep from punching something, namely Felix Dowd. What Drake and I had together had been wonderful and real and pure, not the tawdry mess this asshole made it out to be. A brief image of Drake in the car last night, injured and alone, made my heart ache. I prayed he was okay and that he'd figure out the clues I'd left him before it was too late.

I took a deep breath and tried to concentrate on what I had to do here to stall. I needed time to wake up, find the phone, listen to the recording, then contact the authorities. A quick glance at the digital clock above the professional-grade stove said I had about an hour before Jameson showed up to work in accounting and began to see all those withdrawals from the foundation's accounts. Withdrawals I'd linked to Drake's name.

If we both got out of this alive, I owed Drake some big-time apologies. For not telling him the truth about my past. For creating evidence against him, even if I only did it to save his life. For not being honest about how much I loved him and wanted to be with him, wherever the future might lead.

But I might never get the chance now. Too little, too late.

I swallowed hard and switched subjects to one I knew Felix Dowd liked to talk about the best—himself. "Why'd you work with Devon?"

At first Dowd didn't respond, just held my gaze for a moment. Then he sat back and picked up his tea again, sipping it, then watching me over the rim. "I know what you're trying to do, Miss Turner. Buying time." He looked over at the clock, then back to me. "But I suppose it can't hurt for me to monologue a bit, right? I did come up with a brilliant plan, after all, and it would be a shame not to share it with someone who can appreciate it, especially since you won't be around long enough to share it with anyone." Dowd laughed and shook his head. "You may be right, my dear. I do sound like a movie villain. Sorry. Too much work and no play. Maybe I'll take a nice vacation in South America after this. Get some R and R. Refocus my mind."

I had several ideas of what he could do with his mind, and the rest of him, but refrained from saying so. As long as the guy kept talking, it bought Drake another minute to find the truth and find me.

"Anyway," Dowd said. "I began working with Devon Shepperton shortly after his parents died. He'd taken over the company as CEO and was looking to expand Shepperton, Inc.'s holdings internationally. I had extensive connections in Eastern Europe and offered to help him make some acquisitions there. The Baltic region was in flux then and grabbing land rights was almost too easy, if you knew what you were doing."

"And you did?"

"I always do."

His chilling grin made me shudder. I wrapped my thin black cardigan tighter around me. "What about Carrie Bartlett? How'd she fit into all this?"

"Just a very minor cog in a huge machine. Expendable. So expendable."

My eyes widened as the ramifications of that word hit home. Before I could ask him if Carrie Bartlett was dead, he continued.

"Anyway, after getting my hands on a couple of lucrative oil and natural gas reserves in Belarus, I approached Devon about partnering with me on them. He, of course, was thrilled. At least until I laid out my terms for co-ownership. We couldn't funnel the money directly into our bank accounts because of laws and sanctions, so we had to get creative with the financing."

"Creative." My heart sank as I put the pieces together. "That's why you used the foundation."

"Yes. Very good, Miss Turner." He finished his tea and set the empty cup aside. "No sense dirtying our hands with tainted money, when we could run it through a couple of charities and grants and come out fresh as daisies and with a tidal wave of great PR to boot. The local chamber of commerce even gave me a medal last year, did you know that? Philanthropist of the year." Dowd shook his head again and laughed. "Idiots."

I felt like the biggest idiot of all, though, for not seeing all of it sooner. I'd tried so hard to be different, to not follow in my parents' footsteps, and yet I'd inadvertently ended up exactly like them. Even if I'd been a dupe rather than an accomplice, I still blamed myself. I'd run the foundation; I should have known what Devon was doing, should have questioned him more. But nope. I'd fallen for his BS hook, line and sinker.

Idiot indeed.

Before I could fall too deeply into my pit of despair, however, the door leading out onto the exquisitely manicured back lawn opened and a well-armed man dressed all in black entered. He rushed to Dowd's side and whispered something to him that I couldn't catch.

Dowd's expression hardened slightly before relaxing back into an unreadable mask. He murmured a response to the man, then stood as the guard headed back outside. "Excuse me, Miss Turner. There's something I need to deal with. I suggest you get back to your room and stay away from the doors and windows."

My blood froze. "What? Why? What's going on?"

Felix Dowd came around the island and took me by the arm, muscling me to my feet and down the hall toward the stairs with far more force than I would have given him credit for. "Get upstairs. Now! I don't have time to argue with you. If you want to stay alive, you'll do as I say." When I hesitated again, he shouted, "Go!"

I'd barely made it to the second floor, however, when the sound of shattering glass echoed from the foyer below. Then all hell broke loose. Bullets flew everywhere. Men shouted and doors crashed in. I tried to take cover as best I could while the world exploded around me, ducking to shield my abdomen and protect the twins. They were all that mattered now. I'd screwed up my own life, despite my best intentions. Had lost the man I'd loved. Had made the wrong choices…

Footsteps pounded up the stairs amidst shouts of "FBI! Put your hands up!"

I covered my head and pushed farther into the corner, dizzy and distressed and downright terrified. I should have taken Dowd up on his offer of toast in the kitchen. I'd not eaten since lunch the day before and now I was lightheaded. Not good considering the shitty situation around me now. I cowered even more, unable to stop the violent tremors racking my body.

"Hey," a deep male voice said from somewhere close. "Layla, sweetheart?"

Great. Now I was hallucinating. What came next? Coma? Death?

I flinched, hugged my arms tighter around my legs, cradling my stomach. No. I wouldn't die. The twins needed me. The twins deserved a happy life.

Happy. I would have been happy with Drake. In a perfect world, we could have had the most amazing future together.

"Layla?" the voice said again and this time a gentle hand clasped my arm, pulling me out of the corner and forcing me to look up. "Sweetheart? Please say something. Please tell me you're okay."

At first, I didn't believe my eyes. I blinked, then blinked again. As the handsome face swam in my vision, tears welled and spilled down my cheeks. Before I could stop myself, I'd thrown my arms around Drake's neck and held on like I'd never let go.

"I'm sorry. I'm so sorry," I sobbed against his neck, not caring how it looked. Not caring that this wasn't me. I wasn't usually a crier, but today—God. Today, I was. "Please don't leave me. Please."

"Shhh," he soothed me, stroking my hair and holding me close. "I'm not going anywhere, sweetheart. I promise."

He rocked me slowly for a while as the chaos gradually ended downstairs. I had no idea how long we sat there on the floor, but finally Drake's strong arms lifted me, carrying me down the stairs and outside into the backyard. The sound of chirping birds and leaves rustling finally had me lifting my face to look at him. Dark circles marred the skin beneath his eyes and there was a purple bruise and cut in his temple where the thugs had knocked him out the night before, but damn. I'd never seen anyone more beautiful in my life. Drake walked over to a stone bench near the perimeter of the yard and sat down, ignoring the agents running around the place, arresting people and collecting evidence. I barely registered when they marched Dowd out of the house, handcuffed and tight-lipped in his ugly silk robe. I only had eyes for the man on whose lap I sat.

Drake cupped my cheek and stroked my skin with the pad of his thumb. "Please tell me you're okay."

I nodded, not trusting my voice at first. Finally, I croaked out, "I'm fine."

"I was so worried about you," he said, hugging me tightly again and burying his face in my hair. "You are so brave, so amazing."

His words only made me cry harder. I wasn't any of those things. "I'm sorry you got hurt. I'm sorry I said those awful things last night. I didn't mean any of them. I never meant any of it."

"I know, sweetheart. I know."

We held each other for a while, until finally I leaned back to ask, "You're not angry? About my past?"

He snorted. "Seriously? How could I be when I've spent the last decade distancing myself from my own family? You did what you had to do to survive. We both did. When you had the chance, you made the right decision—you testified against them, and put your life on a new trajectory. One that brought you to me. That's what matters." He kissed me lightly. "And you kept me from getting shot, so yeah. Grateful all around, really. Thanks, Layla Bailey."

I sniffled and swiped the back of my hand across my damp cheeks. "Turner, actually. Bailey is my grandmother's maiden name. My real name is Layla Turner. I hate it, though, so I don't use it."

"Well." Drake clasped his hands behind my lower back. "If you dislike it that much, you could always change it permanently. Layla Shepperton has a nice ring to it, I think."

It took a minute for that to sink in. When it did, I frowned up at him. "What are you saying?"

"I'm saying that I love you, Layla Bailey. Or Turner. Or whatever you call yourself these days." He sighed. "I know we agreed to keep things temporary between us, and at first, I was okay with that. But the more time we spent together, the more I realized that my priorities were changing. I want a future with you, with the twins, right here in Dallas. I want to build a new life with you. A new phase in my life."

"What about your SEAL team?" I asked, still wary of this thing between us. I loved him too, but old habits died hard. Happiness was a hard thing to trust, after the life I'd had up to now. "You love traveling and being on missions."

"True." He nodded. "I do love that stuff. But being back here, with you, brought back lots of memories from my past. Made me realize that at one time, I'd dreamed about making the future better, not just for myself, but for my community. The best way for me to do that is by keeping Shepperton, Inc. and starting it on a new path."

"Wait." I scooted off his lap to sit beside him on the bench, keeping hold of his hand just because it felt so good to touch him again. "You're keeping the company?"

"Yes. There are too many people dependent on it, on me, for me to turn my back on it now. I joined the SEALs because I wanted to make a difference, but staying here will allow me to make lasting, real changes right here in my own hometown." He kissed my hand, then met my gaze, his dark eyes glittering with intent. "But only if you're by my side, Layla. I'm asking you to be my partner, my lover, my wife. What do you say?"

I opened my mouth to answer and promptly burst into tears again. Maybe it was the pregnancy hormones. Maybe it was the stress of the night before and the raid this morning. Maybe it was the fact that I'd been strong and independent and self-reliant for so long that I feared I'd never find my counterpart. Yet here he was. Drake Shepperton. Offering me everything I ever wanted and exactly what I needed. A true partner, someone I could trust. A shoulder to lean on and a hand to hold, through thick and thin, whatever might come our way.

I wanted desperately to say yes, but something held me back from accepting. I wasn't sure what was happening. All I knew for sure was that I couldn't seem to think straight at the moment. I buried my face in his chest, the steady beat of his heart beneath my ear calming me.

"Is that a no?" he said, chuckling. "'Cause it seems like a no."

"Yes," I said, then sat back. "I mean no. I mean, I don't know." At his disappointed look, I said, "I can't think straight right now. I'm so—"

Drake put a finger over my lips. "Enough apologies. Let's get you to the hospital first and we'll talk later, okay?"

I nodded, leaning against him again as he carried me toward the waiting EMTs at the ambulance nearby and the last words I heard before I fell asleep were him saying, "She's pregnant, with twins…"

TWENTY-FIVE
DRAKE

"Everything looks fine on the ultrasound," the ER doctor said a few hours later, and I felt like a huge weight had been lifted off my shoulders. I gave Layla's hand a reassuring squeeze, then kissed her knuckles for good measure. "Do you want to know the sex of your babies?"

"Oh, I'm not—" *the father*, I started to say, but she gripped my fingers tighter, stopping me. Drake's My flew to Layla's and she shook her head.

"No, we want to be surprised," she said to the doctor. "Thanks for putting our minds at ease, though."

"My pleasure," the woman said, wiping the gel off Layla's skin and moving the ultrasound machine back against the wall. "Let me get your discharge paperwork ready, then I'll be back in to go over final instructions with you, okay?"

"Okay." Layla sat up with my help, then pulled her shirt back down to cover her stomach. In just the few short weeks we'd been together, her baby bump had become more pronounced, and I felt even more protective toward her, if that were possible.

Honestly, when I'd burst into that house earlier for the raid, I'd been ready to shoot first and ask questions later—whatever it took to ensure Layla and the twins got out of there alive and well. Now that the adrenaline had burned off, though, I felt itchy and unsure. I'd probably pushed it way too far in the garden, blabbing about my feelings and my plans and then asking her to marry me while she sat there, staring at the house of the man who had kidnapped her because of the misdeeds of my own brother. Lord. If I'd ever had any game to begin with, it had disappeared the moment I'd found her cowering in that corner at the top of the stairs, shaking and scared. I'd wanted nothing more than to hold her forever and never let her go, but this wasn't about me now. If she stayed, the decision had to be hers.

I sat back in my seat, still holding her hand, and checked my phone with the other. We'd already been here three hours, between the exams and giving our statements to the cops and filling out all of the paperwork. I was running on empty, and I couldn't imagine how tired Layla must be. She looked far too pale for my liking, but at least one of the nurses had gotten her some juice and crackers to nibble on while we'd waited. And the twins were fine. Thank the Lord, the twins were fine.

I punched in my passcode with one thumb, then squinted down at the missed call notification onscreen. Baron Bexler had apparently called while I had been at Dowd's place during the raid.

Ugh. My first inclination was to put off calling Bexler back until after I'd gotten some sleep, but I might as well handle it all now and get it over with. I hit the redial button and waited for the call to pick up, aware of Layla watching me the whole time.

"Shepperton?" Bexler said after answering on the second ring. "I just saw news reports of a raid on Felix Dowd's estate. They're saying he's been picked up on fraud charges related to the Shepperton Foundation?"

I took a deep breath. "Yes. It's true. My brother got involved in some illicit activities, but I'm cleaning up the mess now."

"Good, good," Bexler said. "That isn't why I called, though. I wanted to discuss our meeting next week. I'd rather skip the introductory stuff we'd originally discussed and get straight into the acquisition process. I've already contacted my attorneys and they are drawing up plans as we speak, so—"

"Actually," I said, glancing over at Layla, "Shepperton, Inc. is no longer for sale."

"What? Why?" Bexler asked, his tone obviously confused. "If you're looking for more money—"

"No. It's not the money." I let go of Layla and scrubbed one hand over my face, sitting forward to rest my forearms on my knees. If I didn't hear another word about money again today or for the foreseeable future, I'd be just fine. "I've decided to stay in Dallas and run the company myself. Rebuild my family's legacy the right way. I'm sorry if that disappoints you, sir, but I feel I owe this to myself and to our employees."

"No, not disappointed," Bexler said. "Well, not for the reasons you think, son. But I'm glad the company will stay in good hands. If you ever change your mind, you know how to reach me."

"I do." I smiled. "But I won't. Thank you again for your offer."

I ended the call, then exhaled slowly before looking back at Layla over my shoulder. She was still watching me, her expression inscrutable. "What?"

"Nothing."

"Don't lie." I yawned then sat back once more. "You knew I was keeping the company. I told you back in the garden."

"Yes." She shrugged, staring down at her hands clasped over her stomach now. "I guess I just wasn't sure if I should believe it."

"Why? I've never lied to you before."

Layla winced and I cringed.

"Look, I meant what I said at Dowd's house." I inhaled deeply. "All of it. I love you, Layla. And I'd love to spend the rest of my life with you. I'm staying here in Dallas and making a go of it. If you want to stay here with me, the invitation is open." Scratching the back of my head, I tipped my head back toward the ceiling. "Honestly, I could use your help."

She snorted. "What could you possibly need my help with? I'm guessing the feds will shut down the foundation, so there goes my job. And you've already got a full staff in place otherwise."

"True. But maybe you could just, I don't know. Take it easy for a while, gestate my nieces or nephews. Maybe one of each."

"Gestate your what?" This time she laughed outright, and my universe brightened. God, I loved the sound of her laugh. Loved everything about her really, even if she'd never love me back. "What a way with words you have."

"Only with you, sweetheart." I took her hand and kissed it again, happiness fizzing inside me like champagne despite the fact that my whole world now seemed topsy-turvy. "Only with you."

Silence fell while we waited for the doctor to return. I didn't know what else to say. I'd laid it all out there, put my heart and future on the line. It was her choice from here. I had to find a way to be okay with that.

Finally, just when I despaired she'd tell me no, she sniffled and looked at me again. "Okay."

I pursed my lips, letting that hang there a second. "Okay what?"

"Okay. I'll help you."

"With the company?"

"With everything." That unreadable expression of hers dissolved into tears once more, and I was out of my chair and pulling her into my arms before I even realized what I was doing. "I'm sorry," she said, against the front of my now tear-damp shirt. "I swear I'm not usually like this. I just can't seem to stop crying today."

I grinned into the top of her hair, then kissed her scalp, inhaling her sweet floral scent. "You could blame it on the pregnancy."

She smacked me on the arm, then laughed again. "I wish I could, but I think you just broke me."

I frowned and pulled back. "I broke you?"

"Yes. Before I met you, I had things under control. I had a plan. I didn't start sobbing every two seconds. I was a rational, independent woman. Then you went and had to be all dependable and trustworthy and make me fall in love with you and…"

Layla buried her face in my shirt again and I was too stunned to stop her.

"Wait. You love me?" I asked after I'd taken that in.

"Of course, I love you. How could I not? You're damned near perfect, damn you."

Joy pulled me under like a riptide and I kissed her, hard and fast and deep before she could change her mind. "You love me, and you're going to help me."

"Didn't I just say that?" She shook her head and gave me a wobbly smile. "I love you, Drake Shepperton, and I want to be with you. Forever and ever, amen. Is that clear enough?"

"Crystal," I said, kissing her once more.

END OF PROTECTING HIS BROTHER'S BABIES

SEAL TEAM FOUR BOOK 2

SEAL's Surprise Daughter

Protecting His Brother's Babies

Protecting His New Family

The SEAL's Convenient Marriage

SEAL's Christmas Daughter

SEAL's Justice

Do you love sexy Navy SEALs? Please keep reading for a preview from my books, **Protecting His New Family** and **The SEAL's Convenient Marriage**.

THANK YOU!

Thank you for choosing my book.
If you're keen to read more heart-pumping, fast-paced romances by me,
then please help me, by leaving an honest review.

Want sexy military men straight to your inbox? Then sign up to my
mailing list at:
www.leslienorthbooks.com/katie-knight

ABOUT KATIE

It isn't a big surprise Katie Knight ended up writing romances about the stellar, studly men of the Navy SEALs; after all, she was a K-9 trainer for the SEALs and met her own Navy SEAL hero husband while preparing one of their K-9 partners for combat. A few years after their marriage, her and hubby decided to retire with their K-9 partner, Sam, to raise their children in the Midwest. It wasn't long after that before Katie decided to write her own stories featuring the men of the SEAL teams and the women who love them.

When not imagining dangerously romantic scenarios for her heroes and their feisty heroines, Katie enjoys hikes with her husband and Sam, spending time with her children, and long runs (on and off the beach).

To learn more about Katie you can check out all her books on social media and her website: www.leslienorthbooks.com/katie-knight

ABOUT LESLIE

Leslie North is the USA Today Bestselling pen name for a critically-acclaimed author of women's contemporary romance and fiction. The anonymity gives her the perfect opportunity to paint with her full artistic palette, especially in the romance and erotic fantasy genres.

Find your next Leslie North book visit LeslieNorthBooks.com or choose:

PS: Want sneak peeks, giveaways, ARC offers, fun extras and plenty of pictures of bad boys? Join my Facebook group, Leslie's Lovelies!

BLURB

My priority has always been serving my country as a Navy SEAL.

But then my world is turned upside down and suddenly I have an adorable toddler to look after.

I won't be doing it alone—my sister-in-law Sam has joint guardianship.

But playing house with this firecracker of a woman is anything but child's play. It's been hard enough to ignore the electric chemistry between us at family gatherings, and now we're living under the same roof.

Hell Week was easy in comparison to keeping my hands off her.

I can't get distracted by the sparks between us though, but doing so may be my toughest mission yet.

When Sam's medical research work leads to growing threats against her, the safety of my new family is put in danger.

Now I'm ready to protect them—to protect what's *mine*, at any cost.

Grab your copy of *Protecting His New Family*
Re-released on May 7, 2024
www.LeslieNorthBooks.com

EXCERPT

Chapter 1: Owen

"Owen, are you sure this is what you want to do?" my baby sister, Katherine, asked over the phone. "I mean…we're all reeling a bit. I can't believe Carter and Lauren are gone."

"Neither can I," I said. My stomach twisted itself into a knot.

"They were far too young." Katherine's voice expressed the anguish our whole family felt, but she couldn't know how her words sliced through me.

She probably thought she was being helpful, commiserating with me, but every word she said made the pain and guilt surge stronger until my mouth filled with saliva like it did before I threw up. This was all my fault.

If I hadn't gone on that date and lost track of time, if I had been where I was supposed to be, if I'd picked them up from the club when I said I would, they would have been out of there before the fire started. They would still be alive. There was only one way to even begin to atone, and he was sitting in front of me, smiling. I restacked the blocks Myles had just knocked over and tried to smile at him when they crashed back to the floor, sending my nephew into fits of giggles.

"I'm sure about leaving SEAL Team Four," I said, returning to Katherine's question. "I filed the paperwork yesterday to resign my position due to hardship." Leaving after all of the loss I'd suffered was the easy part. Becoming a civilian and a dad was far tougher, but it was the reality of my life. I was now the guardian of a fourteen-month-old, and he deserved everything I could give him.

"I can hear Myles giggling. I'm glad he can be happy. I hope he doesn't miss…" Katherine trailed off. Despite being a thousand miles away, Katherine got it. We were all worried about how Myles would adjust to suddenly having his parents taken from him. "I wish I could be there with you for all of this and not just for a few days for the Celebration of Life."

"You've worked too hard to get into Juilliard to give up your dream," I argued, well aware of the hours of rehearsal, the lessons, and the summer camps Katherine had completed to attend the prestigious arts school.

"I know. I just feel…at least Mom and Dad will be there soon to help you."

"Yeah," I said, though I wondered how "helpful" they were going to be. They were the helicopter type, with a tendency to descend on a situation and take it over. As the middle child, I'd been lucky since the focus had largely been off me. As the "oops" baby, born when I was seven and Carter was eight, Katherine had gotten the brunt of it. Then, when her musical gifts had developed, our parents had focused on making sure she had the training she needed to succeed. When she was accepted to Juilliard in New York City, my parents moved to Brooklyn to be near her and still tried to manage her life. I knew she struggled with that since she was twenty-one and wanted her independence.

Mom and Dad's focus would shift to me and Myles now, leaving Katherine on her own. In the four days since the accident, Mom and Dad had already committed to returning to Alabama to "help" me with Myles. In other words, they didn't trust me to care for the toddler and wanted to be close at hand to swoop in when I screwed up. I blew out a frustrated breath, having no delusions about my parents' motives. Nothing was going to be easy for a long while, but this wasn't about me. It was about giving Myles as much care and love as possible. More people meant more love, right?

And then there was Sam. "I'll have Sam here, too," I said to Katherine, pushing away thoughts of my overbearing parents. Lauren's sister, Samantha, had been named co-guardian for Myles along with me.

"How is she doing?" Katherine asked.

Sam's life was as upended as everyone else's. She'd lost her sister and become a mom overnight at a time when her medical research was apparently taking every minute of her time. She'd sounded pained and stressed the handful of times I'd spoken with her. It was a sensation I could identify with.

"Not sure. I've only talked with her on the phone so far. She's dealing with subletting her apartment and something with her work. Once that's squared away, she'll be moving in—and we'll actually start co-parenting together."

"And you're going to be okay living with her?"

"I have to be," I declared, hoping I sounded more confident than I felt. Samantha Mayfield was a problem. A beautiful dark-haired, blue-eyed, smart as hell problem, who I'd once tried to pick up while in a drunken haze. Damn.

"I know you had a thing for her." Leave it to my sister to have a good memory.

"Thanks for reminding me." It wasn't like I hadn't thought about that plenty in the past days. Sam and I decided on that first chaotic day after the deaths that it would be best for Myles to stay in his home for now. Less upheaval for Myles and safety in numbers for the clueless adults trying to figure out how to be parents. Good for everyone, at least in the short term, but it meant Sam and I were going to live in Carter and Lauren's house together for the next several months until we worked out a permanent custody arrangement.

"You're over her though, right?" Katherine had always known how to dig for information.

"Sure," I answered quickly. I hadn't even seen Sam in two years, and she wasn't my type at all, so I must be over her.

"Uh-oh, you're not." What had my sister heard in my one-word response to make her assume that?

"I'm fine. It's just going to be weird to play house with her." Weird, uncomfortable, awkward. Thankfully she'd never received my drunken text asking her out, since I'd accidentally sent it to my brother. I winced remembering Carter's reaction. He'd threatened to punch me if I went anywhere near Sam. I'd fought with my brother plenty growing up, but I hadn't been willing to push him on this topic.

Ironic, then, that Sam and I were forced together by the terms of Carter and Lauren's will. I'm sure my brother never expected his custody instructions to be necessary. Once again, the unfairness of the situation hit me. It wasn't right that a Navy SEAL died in a goddamn fire. It wasn't right that parents of young children died, ever.

I stroked my hand over Myles's soft brown hair, making him look up at me with a toothy grin. Someday, I'd have to tell him that his parents might be alive if I'd kept my word and not gotten side-tracked by a pretty girl in a bar. *I'm sorry, buddy.*

"It's all for Myles's sake," I said, pulling my thoughts back on target.

"Right, of course. Poor darling."

I could hear the tears in my sister's voice. We'd spoken every day since the fire. Painful calls.

"I've got a lead on a job," I said to distract Katherine. "I wouldn't start for at least a month, but I think it's something I might like." We talked about the security position I was interested in for a few more minutes until we were interrupted by the chime of the doorbell echoing through the house.

"Somebody's here," I said, knowing full well it was Sam. Time to face her and begin this co-parenting thing.

"Okay, I'll see you in a couple days," Katherine said. "Love you, Owen."

"Love you, too." I stood and scooped up Myles, putting him down in the playpen to keep him safe on my way to the door. He wasn't walking yet, but the kid could crawl his way into trouble fast. The next months were going to be…

All my thoughts stopped when I opened the front door. Sam stood there. Had she been that gorgeous the last time I saw her? Her dark hair waved around her shoulders, and her bottomless blue eyes were made more intense by the glasses she wore.

Christ, the next months—make that years—of working closely with her to raise Myles were going to be a challenge for a lot of reasons.

Grab your copy of *Protecting His New Family*
Re-released on May 7, 2024
www.LeslieNorthBooks.com

BLURB

Nothing is more dangerous than falling in love.

There's only one relationship Navy SEAL Nate Shaw is wedded to: his job. For Nate, love is nothing but a losing game; he'll never forget the look on his mother's face when his father left. Now Nate remains unconvinced that marital bliss would ever play a part in his life.

For Emily Edwards, love is everything. But she gave up her dream of a fairytale ending when she adopted Nate's baby brother. Nothing is more important to Emily than her brave cancer-stricken son, however Matthew's lifesaving medical treatment has come at a price.

When Nate offers to marry Emily so that she can access healthcare and free housing to help look after Matthew, she hardly leaps at the chance: a marriage of convenience goes against everything she has ever wanted. As for Nate, he's used to businesslike unions, he wants to support both Emily and Matthew – and it will just be for one year, they decide.

But their arranged marriage is soon put to the test when Emily receives threats from Matthew's doctor; and as the dangerous warnings escalate, so do Nate's feelings for her. Forget playing husband, Nate's duty is to protect Emily – and fast. But can he protect his heart from falling in love in the process?

Grab your copy of *The SEAL's Convenient Marriage* from www.LeslieNorthBooks.com

EXCERPT

Chapter 1

"Slow down," Emily Edwards cautioned as her adopted son zipped past the park bench where she sat. At four, Matthew was as rambunctious as any kid, and he was out-of-his-mind excited about seeing his big brother Nate. But cancer had taken a toll on him, and she didn't want him to be worn out when Nate arrived.

"Moooom," the boy complained, returning to her slowly. "I feel good."

He felt *better* was more likely, since the treatments were proving effective against his Hodgkin's Lymphoma. Thank goodness. She took small comfort when people told her there were worse forms of cancer he could have. He'd been her son for the past two years since his mother—her former boss—died in a car accident, and she didn't want to lose him.

"I'm glad you feel well, but Nate'll be here soon." She tapped Matthew on the nose. "You should save some energy for his visit."

Thankfully, her logic got through to the boy, who took a seat on the shady bench next to her, kicking his legs in the air.

"When will he get here?" Matthew asked thirty seconds later.

"Less than five minutes. He's always on time." Emily couldn't blame Matthew for his impatience. He hadn't seen his big brother in almost six months. Nate had been on a mission with his SEAL team to God knew where. Emily never asked questions about his job; she was just grateful he always made time for Matthew when he was back at his home base.

"What if he doesn't recognize me?" Matthew asked in a small voice, his hand rubbing over his bare scalp, the result of chemo treatments.

"Oh, honey, he'd know you anywhere." She put her arm around Matthew and gave him a kiss. She was filled, as always, with the fierce urge to protect him from anything that might harm him. Cancer had been the biggest foe she'd fought so far, but they were finally beating it. Lately, though, she'd had a new concern—Matthew's doctor. She wished she could re-do the day a few weeks ago when she returned to the cancer clinic after hours, accidentally seeing too much. She shivered, recalling the doctor's threatening words to her.

So now she needed to find a different doctor for Matthew's treatments to continue. Not an easy feat when he was three-fourths of the way through the process and her insurance was so minimal she'd already drained her savings account and the last of Matthew's inheritance from his birth mom. She was down to darn near nothing. It would all work out, she told herself, but the feeling of desperation grew a little each day.

"There he is." Matthew hopped up and dashed toward his big brother, who looked…so damned good. Wow. Even better than she remembered. She'd always found Nate Shaw attractive with his dark hair, chiseled features, and muscular build. But looking at him now…he must be one of the finest looking men to walk this planet. She felt heat rise in her cheeks and had to tell herself again that he was not her type of man and in no way should she be interested in him.

As Nate bent to pick up Matthew, swinging him in the air, his pecs and biceps flexed, making her heart race. The way he carried himself, pure confidence, caught her attention in spite of herself. *This is what happens when you don't make time to date,* she scolded herself. *You start eyeing up men who are totally off-limits.*

"How's my little man?" Nate asked the smiling child.

"Great," Matthew responded, his worries from a few minutes ago totally gone, making her smile. They were adorable together, half-brothers nearly twenty years apart in age, but still so loving and cute.

Emily stood when Nate carried Matthew back to the bench. He gave her a one-armed hug, bringing her in close contact with his aftershave. The scent was fresh, clean, but, oh, so masculine. Her eyes lingered on the word *Helen* in small script on his right bicep. Nate and Matthew's mother's name. Emily had always thought the tattoo was sweet, showing a softer side of the tough Navy SEAL. Helen had been a good woman, a good mom before the car accident that claimed her life.

"How are you doing?" Nate asked after they sat again on the bench. Matthew was on his brother's lap, looking up adoringly.

"No complaints," she said, hiding the multitude of things that worried her. Nate wasn't responsible for those and she had no intention of burdening him. The whole reason Helen had asked Emily—Matthew's nanny at the time—to take custody of her baby was so her eldest son, Nate, could continue the life and career he'd chosen without interference. Emily was just happy he chose to be an active part of Matthew's life.

"Thanks for keeping me informed about this guy." He tickled Matthew in the ribs.

"I'm happy to. Sometimes I'm not sure all my messages get through." She'd communicated faithfully nevertheless.

"Most do. I appreciate them, especially the pictures." His dark eyes focused on her face. They were brown and warm with gold flecks that didn't negate their sharpness.

"I thought you'd like to see how much he's grown." She emailed Nate photos of Matthew as often as she could. Most recently, she'd sent pictures of Matthew's fourth birthday party. She'd wanted to take Matthew and a group of his friends somewhere, but the expense and possible exposure to germs prevented her. They'd had a quiet event at home with two of Matthew's closest friends instead.

"Made my day," he said, sounding sincere.

"I can run really fast now," Matthew told Nate. "I've been practicing. Do you want to see?"

Nate shot Emily a look over the boy's head. She held up one finger, and Nate nodded his understanding.

"Sure," Nate responded, "but you can only do it once. How about you run from here to the swings? That'll be plenty for me to see your speed."

Matthew slid down, flashed a grin at them, and took off running the thirty feet to the swings.

"Thanks," she said when Matthew was out of hearing range. "I'm trying to keep him from overexerting himself, but he's a kid so it's been tough."

"He looks good, better than I expected." Nate watched as Matthew reached the swings and turned to wave to them.

"He's responding well to the treatment." Her eyes stayed on her adopted son. As she expected, the swings had gotten his attention. He plopped down on a seat and began pumping his legs. He'd recently learned how to do it himself and was proud he could get the swing going without a push from her.

"You're still worried?" Nate questioned. She should have known he'd pick up on her apprehension.

"I…yes." She was torn about how much to reveal. After all, Nate would likely only be home a few weeks before deploying again. She could easily hide her concerns, but he had a right to know about the boy's health. "I need to find a new doctor and clinic for Matthew, which isn't going to be easy when a patient is in the middle of the prescribed treatment." She didn't mention how limited her resources were, feeling she'd already said enough. "I'm sure it'll all work out though," she added, attempting a more cheerful tone.

Nate studied Emily's profile as she kept her eyes on Matthew. Her lush red lips and deep-toned skin had been haunting him lately, though he couldn't explain why. He'd known her since Matthew was a baby and never saw her as anything but his kid brother's nanny and then adopted mom. Why now, he wondered.

Emily was beautiful. He'd always known that, but at some point in the past months, his interest in her had shifted until she appeared frequently in his dreams, some of which had been rather…graphic in nature. He'd attributed it to the loneliness he'd felt during his recent mission. The location was isolated, leaving him just his brothers-in-arms to talk to, and most of them were missing the women in their lives. He'd had no one to miss.

Had his subconscious focused on Emily since she was the only woman he had a connection to?

Maybe. But whatever the reason, she was still a beauty, even with the worried look on her face. He shifted on the bench, putting more space between them, and pulled his eyes away to focus on his brother. He had no interest in being caught staring at her.

"It's unusual to switch doctors at this stage, isn't it?" he asked, keeping his tone casual.

"I suppose," she gestured as she spoke, making the gold bangles on her wrist dance, "but I think…I think we can do better elsewhere."

"You think the treatments aren't right?"

"It's not that. Matthew's getting better, but," she paused, seeming to gather her thoughts, "I'm not pleased with the personal interactions."

What did that mean? Nate instinctively fell back on his training to try to read her body language, but all he could see was that she was uncomfortable. He didn't think it was because of him. They'd been friendly from the first, except in his recent dreams where they'd been much more than friends. But she didn't know about those, and she never would. No matter how attractive he found her, she was the happily ever after type, and that was something he wasn't prepared to offer anyone.

"I'm not understanding," he said, hoping she'd elaborate.

She swung her eyes to him. A determined, but sexy edge showed. "You don't need to worry about it. I'm going to change clinics quickly, so Matthew doesn't lose any of the ground he's made. It's my decision to make."

He wouldn't argue with her about that. They'd agreed she'd have full custody—as per his mother's wishes. He'd just started his SEAL training and his mother wanted him to pursue his dream and not feel he had to raise a boy who was just two at the time. But that didn't mean he wasn't interested in Matthew's welfare. He loved the kid, always would. Emily loved him, too, and wanted what was best for him. Which meant there had to be a serious reason to cut ties with his current clinic.

"Is there a problem with the doctor?"

She stiffened ever so slightly, her chin going up. So maybe it was the doctor. His hackles rose, as they always did at any perceived threat to those he considered family. Nate had always had a protective streak a mile wide.

"I'll help you look for a new one," he volunteered. The easiest and most obvious choice was to find someone else to take on Matthew's case. "Anything you need me to do, just ask."

"Thanks. I've got some calls in at other clinics, and I'm hoping to hear back soon. In the meantime, it's good to see him play and be happy."

Matthew had found a cute little girl in pigtails to swing with. If it weren't for his bald head, he would seem like any other kid his age, not one suffering from an illness. Nate had promised himself to spend any extra minute he had with his brother before he had to leave again. "I'd like to take Matthew for the night if that's okay with you. I bet you could do with a break. It can't be easy being a single mom—especially for a kid with special needs."

"It's been…fine," she said.

"But an evening alone would be really fine?" He leaned a little closer to her.

She smiled then, the force of it nearly knocking him back. "I have to admit it would. I don't trust him with many people."

"I'm a government certified protector," he teased, "and his big brother."

"I didn't mean to suggest he wouldn't be safe with you," she responded quickly, "but I'm picky."

"Be as picky as you like but take the night off."

"I…thanks, that would be great," she accepted. "I know he'll be safe, and he'll love spending time with you."

"It's a done deal then."

"I appreciate this. It's been a lot to manage lately."

Nate vowed again that for the time he was home he'd do what he could to help her. Maybe that would get her out of his dreams and back to where she belonged in his life—as his kid brother's mom and nothing more.

**Grab your copy of *The SEAL's Convenient Marriage* from
<u>www.LeslieNorthBooks.com</u>**